A Conspiracy of Goodness

C. P.T. Jennings

Red Feather Press 2013

Cover painting by the author: *The Street,* oil on canvas, 1999.

Copyright © 2011 Caroline Jennings

ISBN: 0615817998

ISBN-13: 978-0615817996

In memory of Robert

CONTENTS

1. BAD DREAMS AND DOWLAND DANCES

A light glimmers in the other room and silhouettes a gaunt figure; the figure comes closer – close enough to see, but Henry can't get a look at the facial features. He thinks it's a man, and there is a stale, rotting smell, paradoxically enticing like the composted ground cover in the forest on the hillside where he grew up. The figure, the shadow-man, clasps him gently but firmly and draws him out of bed, and Henry dresses. He doesn't want to rise and dress and no one forces him to, but he does, and then he and the shadow-man catch the train and before he knows it he is standing in a place four hundred miles southwest of New York, beside the train tracks in Deep River, looking up at the hillside where the house is in which he grew up. He is back where he belongs, the train has gone, the man – whoever he was – has disappeared, has apparently never even gotten off the train. And he knows he will be here forever – *that* is the nightmare.

Henry Oliver hasn't thought of it in years. In 1967, his first year in the dance program at Juilliard, he had dreamed it every night and then had stopped dreaming at all. He excelled in the school; he was important there. He stopped thinking about anything else. He had become a New Yorker and Deep River was behind him. And now, twelve years later, there is always a good excuse for not going back to visit. He phones his mother once a week so she won't have to pay for the call. She whines a little about missing him, but how could she miss him? She doesn't have a motherly bone in her body. They have never liked each other very much, in spite of their shared interest in dance. He has invited her, more than once, to come see him perform, has offered to pay for her trip. She doesn't come. Now, his own dances are beginning to fill the company repertory, to enter the repertories of other companies. He is "up and coming," some people say a prodigy. At first he sent her clippings; after all, she trained him. She says, " well, it's from your father you got your musicality. Not from me. I just taught you the five positions." It's like a shrug. No big deal. He doesn't send her clippings anymore. He was last home in 1975, four years ago. Saigon had just fallen. He was on his way to teach a master class in Pittsburgh and stayed for two days. Excruciating.

And now he is thinking of that ancient nightmare again. He wonders if he has dreamed it during the night; it doesn't seem like he has. He just feels as though he is remembering something from twelve years ago. It stays with him all day, through therapy, through his confrontations - first with Ray, then with Hector – and through rehearsal.

The therapist looks concerned when Henry says the pain isn't much better.

"What does the doctor say?"

"The doctor wants to operate," Henry tells her, "but then, doctors always want to operate, don't they? To me, it's a last resort. I've been dancing for a lot of years – pain is normal."

"You have swelling again," the therapist reminds him, touching the knee. He flinches automatically.

"I want to dance at the opening. Then I'll take a break." She looks at him skeptically and he has the decency not to say, "I promise."

He calls Ray on the phone and has to call back twice before he answers. He hears another voice, dopey with sex, in the background. Henry doesn't bother with a greeting. "Rehearsal starts in exactly 57 minutes. If you're even a minute late this time, you're out. Are you on anything?"

"Christ, Henry. I'll see you later." And hangs up.

Henry opens the fire door and climbs the stairs to the studios, gritting his teeth. Hector comes out of his office just as Henry enters the corridor and before he can subdue the grimace of pain on his face. "Come into my office, Henry."

Without asking if he wants one, Hector pours him a cup of coffee, adds sugar and hands it to him. Henry pretends to take a sip and sets it on top of a book that sits on the edge of the desk: *Modern Dance Forms in Relation to the Other Modern Arts.*

"I'm taking you out of *Still Motion,* and *Fever,*" Hector says. "Your knee isn't up to it."

"Yes, it is. I'm dancing better than I ever have."

Hector holds up his hand. "Don't argue with me. I'm perfectly aware of your ability to pull off miracles, but do you really want to guarantee the end of your dancing career within the next six months?" Henry is silent, and Hector studies him, cups his chin in his right hand. "I see. Well, in that case, the injury is worse than I thought. You notice I've said nothing about *Dowland Dances.*"

"Yes, I noticed," Henry says quietly.

"Well, I think you should give it over too, but it's your love-child – after all you've put into it I hate to say you can't dance. If it's the only one you dance in then there should be less risk of irreparable damage." Hector shakes his head. "Can't you be satisfied with just having made the damn thing? After this, you're going to be part of the canon – that should be enough for you."

Henry starts to rise. "Somehow it's not. This piece especially – I have to dance it. I'll rest after."

"Immediately after the opening," Hector says firmly, and Henry acquiesces.

"Yes. Stanton can take over my role."

"There's one other thing. Ray Smiley."

Henry sinks back down into the chair. "He promised he'd be on time today."

"Who else knows his role?"

"Stanton does. Robert, and Enrico."

"Good. I'm getting rid of Ray today," Hector says. "You don't see it Henry – he's not dancing well. He's a substance abuser, to put it mildly – he needs rehab. Even if he goes into rehab and comes out clean I'm not sure that would be enough – he has too many outside interests. Our budget's too tight to keep him on out of kindness."

"I made that role on him," Henry says. "*For* him."

This time Hector stands up, indicating the end of their conversation. "Don't be sentimental, Henry. Honestly, I wish you'd never met him. He's nothing but trouble, and I wouldn't have taken him on if you hadn't been the one to drag him over here. You should have left him in that small-time company where you found him. It's a pity – he's marvelous to look at. But I've made up my mind, and I'd think you'd be relieved too. You can go. Talk to Stanton and the others. I'll be in after I've dealt with Ray."

The rehearsal is hell, because the whole time in the back of Henry's mind is that horrible old dream about Deep River, giving an inexplicable context to what is going on in the front of his mind. He *is* relieved, he realizes angrily, not to have to nurse Ray along anymore in the fear that his dance will be ruined by some unpredictable Ray "moment." It will all be so much easier with Stanton, Robert or Enrico. Uncomplicated. He is exhausted by the end of the day, both his knee and his frontal lobe are throbbing. He just wants to go home and sleep.

Ray is waiting outside. He has pulled his motorcycle up under the entrance overhang, which is illegal. "You bastard, you prig" he says. "I was *early*. Five minutes early. Why did you do it?"

Henry shakes his head. It is beginning to drizzle, prelude to another downturn in the temperature. It has been an unusually cool June. He thinks he might just lean against the pillar and close his eyes. "I didn't do anything. Hector did it."

"Yeah I noticed that. You could have at least had the guts to tell me yourself."

Henry forces himself to look at Ray. He has on his black leather jacket, and the collar is turned up so that fringes of his golden hair are caught along its edges. As

Hector says, he's marvelous to look at. Pipsqueak southern hoodlum turned ballet dancer. Henry has long since inured himself to the effect, except now, to his horror and even through the pain radiating from his knee, he sees the tears balancing on the edges of Ray's lower lids. He looks away.

"I didn't do anything," he says again. "Hector had already decided. I can't help you anymore, Ray. Leave me alone." He walks quickly toward the subway without looking back.

The phone is ringing when he arrives at the apartment, but he ignores it and goes straight to the bed, takes off his shoes and jacket, stretches out on his back. He wants to sleep but can't. He *is* a bastard; he *is* a prig. He's good at his work, but with people, he screws everything up. He knows Hector is right, that he shouldn't dance, but it's just this one performance, then he'll rest. It's for his father. The piece is dedicated to him. The program is going to say, "to Max."

The phone begins to ring again. Probably Ray. He remembers the day he met Ray. That was a fun day.

He held out his hand, smiling, and Henry took it. He looked familiar, but Henry couldn't place him.

"Ray Smiley," he said. "I don't guess you remember

me. We were at Juilliard at the same time – I didn't have quite your star-power though - and I auditioned for Hector Gardner coupla years ago..." He shrugged his shoulders. "I dance with the Rose Jewitt Group." It was a respectable company that toured a lot; Henry wasn't crazy about Rose Jewitt's choreography, but the dancers were good.

"I remember you," Henry said, pulling his feet from where they were stuck in the rungs of the barstool. "I saw you dance downtown last year."

They didn't talk about dance. They talked about where they came from, Memphis and Deep River, and about music. Ray liked Mississippi John Hurt, the Cadillac Cowboys, Furry Lewis.

"See? I don't like modern music either. Elvis is as modern as I get. That's the music of my soul, man. Of where I come from." He chided Henry for not listening to mountain music. He knew a lot more about it than Henry did.

He shook his head, ' that's *yer* music; how the hell did you ever get turned on to stuff like John Dowland? Blind Alfred Read, he was from West Virginia. Did you ever hear that song, *Why do you bob yer hair girls/, you know it isn't right/ to cut the hair God gave you/ it is an awful sight* ? You should set some dance on that; it'd be a hoot - it'd make yer career." His hand came down on Henry's shoulder. "Sorry, Henry. I love your work. But –

Dowland? What about Hank Williams? He died in West Virginia. Oak Hill, West Virginia, back seat of a car, at a filling station. You could make a real tragedy out of that. Beautiful. What about Ralph Stanley, Doc Watson?"

His looks were a complete contrast to his personality, as though before leaving Memphis, in order to survive, he had adopted an attitude that would help him seem more masculine. But it contrasted so strongly with his elegance that it only made him that much more exotic. No wonder he left Memphis, Henry thought, but when he said so to Ray, Ray just laughed.

"You've never been to Memphis," he said. "I'm no big deal there, the place is full of weirdos. The weirdest of the weird, even the people in Germantown, where all the rich folk live. It's the humidity. And the kudzu. It'll grow thirty feet in one night, you can watch it growing. So we all drink and watch the kudzu eat the landscape and listen to the blues. It makes us *love* one another." He threw back his head and roared. When he had stopped laughing he looked at Henry, and his expression changed to something almost tender.

"But not too many boy dancers in Memphis, I admit. Don't you think it's funny how many of us southern boys end up here? Southerners *lo-ove* New York City." Henry did not demur when he felt Ray's hand on his knee.

"I'm not a Southerner," Henry said. "West Virginia isn't the South, people don't get that."

9

"Oh I get that," Ray said. "Do you smoke dope?"

It hadn't lasted long. It was the dance connection that remained, Henry told himself.

That incessant ringing. Henry sits up on the edge of the bed to look at the clock. 10:30. Defeated, he picks up the receiver.

Pete Mays is driving home from the school and sees Bella Oliver walking unsteadily along the side of the road, so he pulls over, stops, gets out of the car, and joins her without speaking. He walks along with her for a little way; it is such a snail's pace that it won't put them far from the car when he finally offers her a ride. She loves those few minutes from when the car slows and pulls over to when he finally suggests he drive her up the hill. She's pretty sure that she chooses this time of day to go to the post office because she'll be more than likely to run into Pete. It happens regularly now, twice a week. Tuesday and Friday. Today is Friday.

"Well, Bella, why don't I drive you home?" His hand is under her elbow and he guides her back to the car. When they get to the top of the hill he walks her to the house and comes in for a cup of tea. She offered him sherry the first time and found out he doesn't like it. "But you go ahead," he said, and still says, every time.

They have become good friends. She is talking about Henry.

"Henry was five when Max died," she tells him. Pete balances the little teacup on the threadbare arm of the sofa and watches Bella pour more sherry into her delicate glass. There are old things in this house, pretty old things that someone must have treasured, only Bella didn't treasure them; she used them and broke them and spilled on them, and joked about it. "They belonged to Max's family," she said one time when she noticed him looking. In his house growing up there were always new things, the cheapest possible. Now that it really was his house, he thought about trying to spruce it up, getting some nice things, but it always made him feel guilty.

"That was when I opened the dance school," Bella says, " just before Max's death. Henry was five. Well, I had to do something, didn't I? It wasn't the money; it was the boredom. I took Henry with me and gave him his toys and books to keep him occupied, but, what do you know, the second time, there he is in the back of the class behind all the little girls doing everything that I tell them to better than they do. I ignored him, but then the next time there he was at the front.

"What do you think you're doing, Henry?" I asked, but when he hung his head and tried to go to the back, one of the older girls stopped him.

""He's not doing anything wrong, Mrs. Oliver. He's just too short to be in the back. He can't see." The girls liked him.

"Five years old. Even then, his talent was obvious, but it takes more than talent, and he had that too." Bella sighs, sips her sherry.

"You must have been awful proud of him," Pete says.

"Oh, I don't know. A little. He was such a quiet little boy, reading and dancing and playing the piano."

"Was he different before Max died?"

"No, not really. Later, I just worried people would make fun of him, pick on him. A boy like that, in a place like this."

"It didn't happen though," says Pete. He remembers Henry from high school and recalls the little prose gloss in Part IV of *The Ancient Mariner*: the lords that are certainly expected and yet there is a silent joy at their arrival. Whenever he teaches Coleridge, he remembers Henry and Jack.

"He could take care of himself," Bella says curtly, and Pete knows not to push for more answers today. So he says, "I'd like to know more about Max."

Her response is a shrill laugh. "Oh, Max. Well now.

Everyone loved Max, didn't they? He came through London on his way home from the war, and there I was, a silly girl. He liked my accent – American men do. And my name – how many American women have you ever known named Arabella?"

Pete smiles. "Nary a one. What was he like? I get this idea he was revered."

"Oh, yes," she says. "Max was brilliant. Henry takes after him completely."

"It must have been so hard for you when he died. A tragedy."

"Of course," she says, pouring more sherry. "I loved him very much." That is true at least. She has often wished she could cut her heart out.

Pete is beginning to feel that there are no safe places. Intemperately, but with uncanny accuracy, he says, "Henry hasn't been home in awhile."

"Well, he's busy. All these accolades and things. Why would he want to come here?"

" It's his home, or was. Do you ever ask him?"

"I don't like to intrude."

Pete was visited by an unfamiliar sense of firmness. "Well, you should. You're his mother. He might want to come home but is waiting to be asked." He stands up, hoping that if he leaves she will stop drinking sherry. It's almost all gone anyway. "I'd better get going - my cat will be wondering where I am. You call Henry and invite him home."

She loves Pete; he gives her courage.

Roy calls the extension on the front of his house a porch, but it's not exactly. When the spring comes, even if it is not really warm enough, he brings outside the old rocker with the seat that is unravelling and sets it to one side of the doorway. On the other side is the straightback chair that is so old and weatherbeaten it isn't worth bringing inside for the winter. And even though it is snowed and rained on unceasingly, bleached and abused by every kind of weather, it still manages not to fall apart. This old chair is a lot like me, Roy thinks, as he shifts his weight to tilt the ladderback against the wall of his house and watches Pete walk up the path as he always does.

"You're late this evening, Mr. Pete," Roy says when Pete is near enough to hear without him shouting.

Pete sits down on the other chair and stares into the trees with satisfaction. "I took Bella Oliver home from the post office, and she made me tea."

"Then I reckon you don't want any of my coffee."

Pete smiles. "Now why would you think that?"

Roy lets the chair back down onto all four legs and pushes himself up carefully. "Well, you'll be up all night."

"It's Friday, and besides, I've got two rolls of film I want to develop."

Pete no longer tries to make Roy call him just plain Pete. He comes from the time when even to call him "Mr." Pete is a privilege; it doesn't matter that Pete is half his age, or that Roy has known him all his life. They have discussed the problem more than once. They can't talk about everything, but this is something they can talk about. Pete's solution is to call Roy "Mr." too, when he remembers.

"Call me whatever you want as long as it's not "nigger," or "darkie." I'm glad times have changed," Roy said one time when they were talking about it. "But it's habit, and I'm an old man. I came to the valley in 1929 from Alabama and this place seemed like the height of tolerance compared to down there. I wanted to work in the tunnel that Virginia firm was building, but they thought I was a local negro. You know what they said? That the local negroes need not apply - they were too uppity. So they took the ones from way down south, from Alabama. Max Oliver's daddy stopped me from telling them the truth. Just come work in the mines, he said. He was right. I may bear a limp from that slate fall, but I'm alive – most of those tunnel workers aren't."

He brings the coffee back, and Pete sips while Roy gets out his Bugler and begins to roll a cigarette. Roy makes his coffee the old fashioned way and by now it's strong as axle grease, but Pete doesn't mind. He's so addicted to the stuff that it takes that to give him any sort of jolt at all. He always stops at Roy's on the way up the path to the house. Not that Roy needs to be checked on – he's different from Bella – but sometimes Pete is a little reluctant to get back to the house.

"I saw Mz. Oliver from a distance the other day," Roy says. "She's lost weight."

"She doesn't say anything, but I don't think she's very well. She doesn't take care of herself."

"No, well. She never did."

"I forgot. You were pretty close to her husband Max, weren't you?"

"Um-hm, pretty close." He licks the paper and rolls the cigarette. It's so thick Pete doesn't see how it stays together, but it does.

"What did you call Max?" Pete asked.

Roy thinks of the past. "Well, now. Sometimes this, sometimes that. That man was a different case."

"Tell me something about him," Pete says. "Bella never will, but to hear people talk he was a kind of hero."

"Hero in the war, that's right. And he stood up for the workers at the plant in spite of being management. You must be about the same age as that son of his," Roy observes.

Pete nods. "We were in school together, but I didn't know him very well."

"He's up there in New York now, doing well, I hear. He ever come home to see his mama?"

"Not recently," Pete says. "She says it's been four years."

The two men are used to each other after six years of living on the same hillside. Pete lives in the house he grew up in. Six years ago, Roy knocked on his door and made him an offer. He said, "Mr. Mays, if you will let me build a little house on your place to live in, I'd help you to look after the property." As he said it he was standing on the front porch of the house Pete had inherited from his father, looking out at the unkempt hillside. He added, "Your retaining walls could use some work." He was someone who enjoyed building walls.

Pete didn't mind the idea; he didn't even have to think it over. He agreed then and there, and within the week Roy had begun his house, one room, out of stone off the mountain, two root cellars hedged into the hillside behind. And now they are sitting on what he calls his front porch – the slab of concrete held in place by the roots

17

of a tree on either side. The slab tilts, giving it somewhat the look of a little boat tacking through vegetal waves. The view from the porch even in June is mostly dense greenery; you can see the road down below, but only a glimpse of the river and railroad tracks. It is quiet. The droning sound of summer hasn't begun.

"I used to know the son," Roy says. "When Max died, I thought I might be able to help Bella and the boy, but she had took against me."

"You called him Max then. Not Mr. Max."

"Seeing your girl tonight, Mr. Pete?"

"She's not my girl; she's just a friend. No." He doesn't like to talk about these things, and Roy knows it. The two men laugh.

After Pete leaves her house, Bella stoppers the decanter and carries her glass and the teacup into the kitchen. She loves Pete's visits, but they always leave her with a faint melancholy, as though she has seen what she wants but can't quite reach it. She knows what causes the sadness: her effort to suppress a wish that *her* son were like Pete – loving, giving, happy to come and visit. She knows it's a bad wish, for all sorts of reasons not the least of which is her own culpability in Henry's distance. She deserves what she's gotten, but maybe that means she deserves – just a little – to have Pete step in like he does, to make her happy.

When she turns on the light in the kitchen, a mouse disappears over the edge of the counter by the sink. It's a mess, as always. The dishwasher hasn't worked in two years, and she's stopped hiding dirty dishes in it because she forgets about them. She was never one of those people who finds hand washing the dishes therapeutic and so waits until she has no choice but to wash them and put them away. Only now, she has so little energy. She sets the two additions on the table, turns out the light, and heads slowly for the stairs. She leaves burning only the little Tiffany lamp on the hall table, and for a moment she stands at the foot of the stairs enjoying the sight of its warm light on the mahogany railing. It's a good old house, really, and in spite of everything she's always liked it. Max had done some nice things for her, after all – like this house. He had made sure that if anything happened, she would have it – be saddled with it, he would undoubtedly have thought - once the company put their properties up for sale.

By the time she reaches the landing she is winded. She makes her way slowly to the bathroom where she leans against the sink and regards her face in the mirror. She is sixty-three but looks ten years older. Smoking and drinking and solitude. She blames herself, no one else. It's only fair. But she's cut back on smoking and drinking, whatever Pete thinks. It's a matter of face – her drinking and her "spunk" go together, so she assumes both in front of other people, but she deals in neither when she's by herself.

After brushing her teeth and dousing her face with water she takes her nightgown from the back of the door and carries it into the bedroom, the one she's slept in, with or without Max, ever since coming here thirty-four years earlier. She has never really missed England, except perhaps the proximity to seashore. Her family was never much for daughters, and her one sister was a natural for taking up the mantle of their mother. Loving caregiver. She was glad to leave that class-driven, hypocritical society, even being from an advantaged family. She hadn't realized until years later how much it had meant to Max. She had thought he just liked her accent, as a sort of exoticism.

She stretches out on the bed. Her tummy doesn't bother her so much tonight, probably because she hasn't eaten since the morning. For years, she hasn't given Max much thought, but lately he's come back to haunt her. Probably just old age, or her version of it. Her life flashing before her eyes. She knows she's dying.

He was in his captain's uniform the first time she met him. He had become friends with her brother Adrian in London and had come down to their house in Dorset for a weekend. Handsome, good-mannered, apparently well-educated, he set out to charm them all, not for her sake she well understood, but for his own. She had been in her mid-twenties.

"And here is Bella, our black sheep," Adrian said as she came into the sitting room where the rest of the family was already gathered. "Been encouraging any strikes lately, darling? For a ballet dancer, she's a little too politically involved. The war's bringing out both the best and worst in our women, I fear. But our Bella knows how to fix the car now – think of it."

"You're a ballet dancer?" Max asked, politely ignoring Adrian's jibes.

"Was hoping to be," Bella said, "but by the time things get back to normal it will be too late for me. I could teach I suppose – although my family doesn't approve of that idea any more than they do of women striking for higher wages."

"And would you let that stop you?" he asked.

That was the moment she decided he was all right "Well, no. I don't suppose I'd let anything stop me if it mattered enough." But that had turned out to be a lie.

It was difficult to get him to talk much about himself. He was the only child of a coal mine operator in the Appalachian mountains, but had gone away to university. "Will you go back after the war, to take up your father's reins?"

Max grinned at her. "Well, I can tell that would meet with your hearty disapproval, coal miners being the sad victims that they are – in this country too. Yes, I expect I'll go back, but not to mine coal. I'm a chemist. I've been offered a good job in the chemical industry there."

He wrote her a letter to say how much he had enjoyed meeting her. Then he disappeared into the brutality of the Ardennes offensive and she didn't see him again until the end of the war. She had lost her job and come down to Dorset to think what she would do next. She was alone except for the caretaker and so was surprised on a Thursday morning to hear a motorcycle and look out the window to see him standing there looking up at the house. She had forgotten how handsome he was. It was easy then, in the empty house, with no job, no career, the chilly indifference of her family, and his clipped American endearments in her ear, to succumb to the romance of it. "I've come to ask if you'll marry me," he said, but there was no mischievous grin as there had been on the first occasion. The war had changed him. The Ardennes Offensive had. He had been attached to a medical unit, and they had given him some sort of medal, but he would never talk about his experiences. From what she had read in the papers while it was going on – all the weeks of ignorance and worry and waiting to hear - she thought she could guess why.

He brought her back to Deep River. They had moved into the house a year later, and Adrian sent her some boxes of things from home. She had told Pete that they were Max's things, but that was a bit of a white lie. Max had fibbed to her about his father being a coal operator, although it was true enough that he had gone away for his university education. His father had been a miner, not an owner. She was the one with family heirlooms.

After awhile, Bella sits up and swings her legs over the edge of the bed. She sits hunched over in the shadows while uninvited images flit through her mind, silly, inconsequential things she hasn't thought of in years. She looks down at her knees and then bends over a little more so that she can see her feet, not quite touching the floor. She still has high arches, even though they've fallen. Perfect dancer's feet. She looks at the glowing hands of the little clock: 9:00. Well, she doesn't usually do it, but Pete might be right. She turns on the light to read Henry's number written in black ink on the cover of the thin phone book. Carefully she dials it making sure to get the long number right. Lets it ring eight times before hanging up. She should have gone up to New York one of those times, to see him dance. Now it's too late.

When Henry picks up the receiver, he hears an

unknown male voice. "Henry Oliver?"

"Yes."

"Do you know a man named Ray Smiley?"

"Who is this?"

"Police. I'm Detective Spence. I'd like to come over and talk to you."

Henry looks down at his swollen knee, points his toes. "All right."

"He is a work colleague. And a friend," Henry says to the stocky middle-aged man who has presented his identity card.

"I'm sorry to have to tell you – he's dead. Looks like a drug overdose, probably deliberate." Detective Spence gauges Henry and pulls an envelope from his pocket. It's a little crumpled. "He left all his papers, will and so forth, out on his kitchen table where they could be easily found. Along with this letter addressed to you. Sorry – we opened it."

Henry takes the envelope and looks down at where the flap has been raggedly torn. He imagines that the warmth of the paper is Ray's warmth, living writing. He doesn't want to read it in front of this man. He doesn't want to read it at all. He looks up at the policeman, who seems to understand his reluctance.

Do you know anything about his family?"

"He's from Memphis, Tennessee. He wasn't close to any of them."

"Well, we knew that."

"What do you mean?"

"His will. He left his possessions to you." He hands him a slip of paper. "That's the lawyer's name and number. And here's my card. We should be done with this quickly – then you can have the keys to the apartment. Do you mind identifying him?" He sees the stark terror in Henry's eyes. "Or do you know someone else who could do it?"

"No. Sorry. I'll do it."

He opens the door. "Dancers, right?"

Henry nods.

"I've seen you," says Detective Spence. "My wife used to drag me to those things, but by god I've come to like it. I don't suppose..." his hand hesitates near his pocket as he comes out in a rush with his incongruous request. "Could I have your autograph – for Jenny?"

Dear Henry,

Whoo-ee, am I high! Penultimate high – only one more step to go. Don't worry, boy, I know what I'm doing.

I just don't want you taking all the credit, you hear? I know you didn't sell me out, the same way I know I always liked you a whole lot more than you liked me. Par for the course, but no hard feelings, I promise.

One favor. Let Enrico do my part at the premiere. He's sympatico, as we southerners like to say.

Ciao, bello-

Ray.

2. RETURN TO DEEP RIVER

On the day of his arrival, Henry walked two blocks from the Kramer train station to the Greyhound bus stop. The buses ran every half hour and went right through Deep River. The driver would let you off anywhere along the way. No one saw him get off in Deep River, but someone had recognized him as he walked from the train station to the bus stop, and word of his return had spread quickly.

He had brought very little with him, a shoulder bag with books and papers and a small suitcase. He stepped off the bus by the Deep River Inn and stood for a moment looking at the Inn, the quiet road, the river where it widened just above the Inn, and then turned to look up the hill toward his mother's house. The June foliage had not yet obscured the hillside and the house was plainly visible. He began the long climb up, at the end of which the pain in his knee had radiated to include his leg and hip.

He let himself in as he always had, at the unlocked kitchen door. The kitchen, pleasant and old-fashioned, was a mess. He left the two bags on the floor inside the door and had to restrain himself from automatically going to the sink to wash the dishes there.

27

"Bella."

He found her dozing on the wooden-armed sofa in the living room. The stoppered sherry decanter sat on the table beside her, nearly empty, alongside four dirty glasses.

Bella's eyes opened. He sat beside her.

"Been having a party?" He asked.

Her eye moved to the table. "In your honor," she said.

He leaned over and kissed her, then stood and began clearing away the glasses.

"So. You're here," she said. "This place needs a good cleaning. How long are you staying this time?" Her voice scraped. She could hardly bear it, the urge to pull his head into her chest and burst out weeping.

He stood holding the tray he'd filled with the dirty sherry glasses and the ashtray and looked down at his mother. I'm almost thirty, he thought, and she's sixty-three.

"I'm thinking of staying awhile," he said.

"*Awhile?*"

"Yes," he said, in exactly her own tone of uncertainty although neither of them recognized it.

"Awhile." Henry didn't know any better than she did what he meant by 'awhile,' so he turned and carried the dishes to the kitchen.

He has been here for a week and during that time has only ventured as far as the little wooded sanctum of his childhood, half way up the hill behind the house. It is the one place where he can afford to contemplate all the reasons he gives himself for returning. The one place where he remembers his ultimate objective, the same one he has always had: to leave.

Sometimes he goes out and sits on the stone retaining wall Roy Bright built. He usually takes a book with him and reads until his buttocks start to ache, something he has liked to do ever since Roy built the wall the summer after his father died. It was a place where he could be unseen by other children. He didn't like them studying him, talking about his father's death.

On this seventh morning of his homecoming Henry sits up and throws the sheet aside in order to swing his legs off the bed. His knee is stiffest and most painful in the morning, so he shoves his thumb into its tenderness, as though increasing the pain will assuage it. He looks down at his thin and graceful body, rubs his hands up the muscles of each arm and feels his eyes burn a little with a polluting mix of negative emotions. Self pity, he thinks, and wills it away. Gritting his teeth he pushes up from the bed and limps to the window to thrust aside the curtain and reveal the view he has known since childhood.

This small room was always his. It is the most poorly ventilated in the house and therefore hot in summer and cold in winter, but the view of the valley is magnificent. He doesn't mind the intemperate heating and is somehow comforted by the room's undesirability.

Up the river, three miles distant, he can see where the two rivers join and disappear into their swaddling of hills. Downstream, the smooth water is broken by the rocks of Kramer Falls and its riot of foam just above The Island, not an island at all actually, but a peninsula which is flooded for several months out of the year. From this high window he can see all of the village of Deep River, is able to peer down into every street, alley, broken sidewalk and scrappy backyard; he can see it all, except for Linda Paisley's house, which is obscured by three gigantic spruce trees.

There is an aggressive scratching sound at the door. Before he can speak his mother pushes her head through the foot-wide opening she allows herself and, seeing her son standing naked at the window, partially retracts it. He knows what she will do next. Over thirty years her behavior toward him has hardly changed He grins in spite of his annoyance.

"Morning, Bella."

She pushes the door wide open and steps into the frame. She looks him up and down defiantly, but her wide face has reddened.

"I don't know why I shouldn't look at you," she says unnecessarily, as she has done countless times. "I saw you that way the day you were born."

"I don't know why you shouldn't either," Henry says. But he has already begun to pull on the tee shirt he had left on the chair the night before.

They are not alike, in looks or anything else. She is small, soft and rounded while he is long-limbed and angular. Rita's hair, once red and lustrous, has faded to straw and is cut short about her ears, a little crookedly. She had gained a few pounds too many in earlier years but is now, Henry notes with a twinge of concern, losing it rapidly, and the reversal makes her skin hang slack. Her clothes, bright and dowdy, enhance her pallor, the one physical characteristic she might be said to share with her son. She looks old. She does not look cared for. And he doesn't have to be told that she is ill.

"Awake finally," Bella says as she moves slowly across to him. She reaches up to push the fine dark hair away from his brow. She stares into his eyes. Max's eyes. "It's nearly nine o'clock. I want you to go to the post office for me, think you can manage that?"

She reaches down to pinch his buttocks and

watches him flinch. She has never been able to resist doing what he can barely tolerate. Pulling away, his eyes cast down, he notices that her feet and ankles are swollen. He opens the top drawer of the dresser to pull out a pair of underpants and she is behind him peering into the drawer.

"Neat as ever, I see," she says as she regards the perfectly folded socks and underwear with a critical eye. She reaches around him and pulls open the lower drawer where his shirts are neatly stacked. There is mocking reproach in her inspection; that has always been her reaction to her son's inherent neatness. When he was a boy, she had let him think that his embarrassment at her own sloppiness amused her. Eventually he had realized that her disorderly housekeeping had made other children feel at home; they never had to worry about messing up her house. It had only added to his sense of being alien.

"So how's the leg today?" she asks, watching him as he limps from the dresser to the bed, where he sits rubbing his knee and looking quizzically up at her. He hasn't the energy to do more.

"About the same," he tells her.

"Why don't you go to Doc Shumate? He'd be happy to see you."

"No need. I'm used to this," he lies. "It will heal in time."

Bella cocks an eyebrow and tilts her head skeptically. The unhealthy look of her disturbs Henry. He had not liked it when she gained weight; he likes still less seeing her lose it in this abrupt way. She had once had a sense of style. Her clothes now hang shapelessly over the inelastic skin.

"He'd still like to see you," she says of Doc Shumate as she pulls a pack of Old Golds from the pocket of her dress.

Henry shakes his head. He draws the line at smoking in his room. She just doesn't know how to resist annoying him.

She returns the cigarettes to her pocket and throws her hands up.

"Okay, okay!" She says and turns to leave. "I'll see you in the kitchen."

He calls after her, "Doc Shumate would like to see *you*."

Henry finds his way, as he always does, to his father's bookshelf. It contains the other legacy, besides his looks, from the man he had barely known, who died when Henry was five years old. It is a compact and high-minded assortment of books, dog-eared and worn long before Henry got to them. He has almost no distinct or specific memories of his father – his visual memories are based on photographs, of a man who might be himself. These books and sheaves of music have become Henry's true memories of him: Homer, Virgil, Ovid, Omar Khayyam, Shakespeare. medieval romances and Renaissance poetry. Petrarch and Dante, in bilingual editions by which Henry taught himself laboriously to read, but not to speak, Italian. An encyclopedia of music. Sheaves of lute music by the great early English composers – Campian, Byrd and Dowland. By Tielman Susato. Bach. In childhood Henry read all of it, both literature and music. By the time he was twelve, his solitary and expansive mind was a warehouse of the stuff, all the more strange and poignant because it was so out of place and time. But until adolescence Henry had no way of knowing that, and by the time he found out just how unusual a child he was, it was hardly reparable. His father's small library was the foundation upon which he built his life. It is now so much his second nature that he does not realize its effect or value, only its eccentricity. When he was first making friends in New York, he entertained them with recitations of Petrarch in hillbilly twang; he no longer does that. For one thing, his twang is now barely perceptible.

He takes his father's Petrarch out to the retaining wall, first stopping in the kitchen to pour himself a cup of coffee. Bella is not there. He knows that she will find him shortly, and he will oblige her by making the trip to the post office. The part of the wall where he chooses to sit is already warm from the sun, and he looks instinctively for snakes before sitting in the smooth dip of the riverbed stone. He does not open the book. It performs the services of comfort, soaking up the heat just as Henry does. He enjoys the reptilian pleasure of warmth on the invisible scales of his body; his eyes narrow to blind slits against the sun, and his hearing is pleasantly dulled by the early summer drone beginning in the stillness of the air. His entire being resists any kind of action, but he has been here a week and knows he must go to the post office sometime. Not only for Bella; he has letters of his own to write and mail.

He had left New York abruptly, although not, to his mind, abruptly enough. Even in his madness, he couldn't entirely forget his responsibility to the company. For an interminable week after Ray's death, he stayed, coaching the dancers, talking to the technicians setting everything up to run smoothly for the premiere. After their first necessary meeting, he avoided Hector in an attempt to forget their shared culpability. He refused to tell him where he was going and at first hadn't known himself. He had thought perhaps Europe, somewhere where no one would know him or find him. Hector was tolerant at first but at last lost patience.

"You can't just leave indefinitely."

"Oh, yes I can. I'll let you know when I know - if I feel like it. My knee hurts, I'm tired, Ray's died, and I think my mother's sick. I have more than ample reason to flip out for awhile, don't you agree?"

"You have a contract."

"Then sue me."

"God damn it, I just might."

It was Bella who decided him. The night after Ray died, he surprised himself by calling her. It wasn't the regular night. "I tried to call you last night," she admitted without even trying to disguise her plaintiveness. He ignores her.

"I thought I'd come see you," he said. "Would that be all right?"

He will put off writing the letters for as long as he can. After all his hard work and accomplishment he has become a coward. He will now lie in the sun like a reptile, turning his face upward toward the sky, toward the truly unknowable heaven whose perverse comfort is its inscrutability; he will let the sun, the real god of heaven, burn right through his head, the skin and bone and tissue of his head , the veins, cartilage, tissue, to sear away the last vestige of provoking thought that prevents his perfect serpentine slumber. And after that, if it still matters, he will write the letters.

He sighs and opens his eyes. He glances toward the house and sees Bella standing silently in the doorway to the kitchen, a worried expression on her simple face. That surprises him. He pulls himself slowly up from the wall, his book in hand, and grins at her.

"To the post office," he announces.

She frowns at the book in his hand.

"You read too much poetry. Just like your father." She turns her back to him and disappears into the dim light of the house.

Bella stands in the shadowy doorway and watches her grown child sunning himself like an old snake upon the stone wall. She stands with one arm leaned into the doorframe and the other, as so often these days, rubbing her agitated tummy. She could watch him for hours and years ago had done so although he didn't know it. She has never quite believed that this beautiful and perfectly coordinated person is a product of her own dilapidated and imperfect self. He was always solemn, even when small - as unlike her as could be imagined. She, with her foolish sense of humor and her inappropriate way of making light of everything, has always embarrassed him. She would have done better with a shallow, outgoing child.

But in his way he had always been content. Now he is not. She stands in the shadows of the doorway and watches him, troubled for him. She can feel Henry's trouble but does not wonder what it is. His life is too unknown to her for that. Once, she might have been able to imagine it; her own dreams had not been so dissimilar, once.

She remembers him as a small boy discovering the shelves of old books. Her impulse had been to read them to him; she had a fleeting mental image of the two of them curled up together on the sofa reading, and then of her explaining to him how his Uncle Adrian had shipped them all the way from the old house in England when it was sold. She would admit that she loved them too. But it was already too late - they were Max's books by then. In one of their quarrels, she had appeased him with the gift of them, and as an affront he had written his name in each and every one. That was the first thing Henry, just learning to read, noticed. He wanted his father in those books, not her, and so she gave him what he wanted. He worried the meanings out of all the strange words, even the ones in other languages, and did not want her help. She found him a piano teacher so he could learn some of the songs in the music books – his mis-singing of the tunes was driving her crazy.

She wanted a child who read *The Hardy Boys*, not Shakespeare. She wanted a child who knew about the things she didn't know, like *The Hardy Boys* or baseball, so that she wouldn't always be confronted with the perverse temptation to correct him when he translated phrases like *gran viaggio* or *dubbiosi scogli* incorrectly. He liked all the things she had given away to Max; all the things that used to be hers but weren't anymore. Half-heartedly, because she was afraid of all those other mothers, she encouraged him to get to know the other children in the neighborhood. Henry brought boys and girls home sometimes, only to grow bored with them, whereas she would warm to them, talk to them, give them things to eat. She had no fear of betraying herself with them, nor did they seem to mind her as Henry did.

She steps out of the shadow and watches as Henry detects her movement and turns his stark gaze on her. He stands up, that damned Petrarch under his arm, breaks into his disarming smile, such a contrast to the look in his eye, and says something she doesn't quite catch.

That is when she frowns and brusquely lies, "You read too much poetry. Just like your father."

He had been a small boy with straight black hair fringing his forehead and getting into his gray eyes. His body seemed all arms and legs then, and there was something wonderful about the way it made him look, as though you just knew he was going to grow into someone special – someone who was beyond her.

She would catch Max studying him. Their looks were so alike that she assumed they must *be* alike. Early, when he was a baby, the idea thrilled her. "Max, don't you want to hold him?"

"Not much," he would say, and go out of her sight. She took it as a joke, male awkwardness at the sight of a helpless baby. But, really, she was not much better. As Henry grew older, Max sometimes took an interest – would take him to the plant if he had an evening errand, or read to him at night, usually from Shakespeare. She could see, even then, how much it meant to Henry.

One night she came and stood on the little landing that led into the living room, with her hand on the doorsill to steady it. Max was in his chair, reading. His chiseled good looks no longer took her breath away. "I want to open a dance school," she told him.

He looked up, and for a moment she imagined he was smiling. "Oh? Why?" he asked. She couldn't see the expression on his face.

Bravely, she stepped off the landing and sat on the arm of the wingchair. "I need something to do. Besides, this valley needs a dance school. I could use the money Adrian sent me and take a loan for the rest."

Max laid his book down and crossed his arms. "You don't make much of an argument. You have something to do – you have a child to raise and a husband to look after. As for this valley needing a dance school – nice idea, but really, Bella, it's *too* romantic. As for the money, who would give you a loan? You have no credit history."

Bella opened the lid to the box where she kept cigarettes, remembered Max's aversion, and closed it again. "You have friends in the bank. You could speak for me."

He seemed to be thinking. "I suppose I could. Or I could loan you the money myself, in return for part-ownership, something like that. Let me mull it over. Don't get your hopes up. I can't imagine what you're planning to do about Henry."

"He's nearly five, and he's a good boy. I'll take him with me. He'll play quietly by himself, or read."

The transaction was completed just four months before Max's death. She agreed to all his stipulations, not really understanding or bothering to decipher the intricacies of their financial arrangement. She found those out later. It had never occurred to her that he saw marriage as a series of business negotiations between labor and management, and that her role was that of labor. She had left her finances to Max since their marriage as wives usually did and trusted him to do the right thing with her pittance from the family estate in England. He had managed to set it up so she had nothing of her own. Max's estate was modest and was to go to Henry eventually. She was to have an allowance and to spend it within the strait-jacket of Henry's house and school.

He had always been unpredictable.

Out of old habit Henry watches for snakes as he limps down the hill and thinks about Bella. She once mentioned that his father taught her the trick of carrying a putter to ward off any troublesome serpents. "Can you imagine me doing that?" He had said no but the truth was Henry could imagine it, Bella swinging the golf club over her shoulder and whacking at some unsuspecting copperhead. But according to her Max had always been the one with the bright ideas, the one to make the suggestions which she then followed. It was Max, too, who chose the house, so high up the mountain that the last yards had to be walked but which gave a splendid view out over half the valley. As a child Henry had feared the snakes and looked forward to cool weather to send them back under their rocks to sleep. In front of Max, he had hidden his fear, having once witnessed his scathing reaction to some timidity on his mother's part. He has wondered what keeps Bella here year after year, in a house that is impossible to care for, in a place where she has never belonged. He asked her once and she pretended not to hear him.

There is some change in Bella besides her deteriorating health. He has always known that her openness was a sham, that all her silliness is something to hide behind. He never believed it; he only found it embarrassing and tolerated it by distancing himself from her. But he senses that she is testing some new water. She has never been maternal and she isn't now. But he wonders if she isn't kicking at one of the walls between them. He doesn't know how he feels about that.

The Deep River post office is housed in one side of the general store facing onto the road that parallels the river. Spreading out behind it and on both sides is the village itself, the narrow lanes either cracked and pitted asphalt or potholed dirt, its fenced houses and yards small but mostly neat, the whole filmed with soot from the ferroalloys plant that Max once ran. The grime is clearly evident even in the lush foliage of summer. The town was built just before 1920, in the heyday of company towns, and it is now an anachronism, like so much of Appalachia. The modest houses are privately owned by families who have a hard time making their mortgage payments. Bella's house on the hill is stately and elegant in comparison to its neighbors in the valley, but that is partly because from down below it would take a pair of strong binoculars to get a good view of it. On his rare visits Henry has noted the gradual deterioration of the place, the need for painting and patching which he finds impossible to discuss with Bella. He has finally come to understand, although she will never admit it to him, that she has no money for repairs, and she will not take money from him. He suspects that the legacy of her well-to-do family was spent long ago. She has social security, from

Max. She never paid the self-employment tax for her dance school in Kramer. It had been too difficult for her to figure out what to do. There was no pension - Max had died too young.

Henry stands in front of the post office and looks back up toward the house. Even from here he can detect suspicious gapes up under the eaves and a worrisome sagging down below, where the house grips the hillside. He makes up his mind to take care of it. That is one thing he can do anyway. He pushes the door open and enters the store. Six pairs of eyes turn to look, and he feels the flush beginning to creep up his neck.

"Well. Speak of the devil," the fat self-satisfied man behind the counter says, and Henry recognizes Ricky Davies. His face is even more bloated, his mouth more trivial, his eyes meaner than in the days of their high school confrontations, and Henry revises his estimate of health considerations for returning to the valley. On his last visit Ricky's father was the postmaster as he had been ever since Henry could remember. He had not liked the elder Mr. Davies either, but there had been no confrontation, only disapproving glares. Henry battles his rising anxiety.

"Hello Ricky," he says as he takes his place at the back of the line. He isn't afraid of him anymore, but he doesn't look forward to a scene. He wonders if that is why he's been avoiding the post office and everywhere else:

fear of scenes. He dismisses the thought and finds himself looking up into the sensitive brown eyes of the man in front of him.

Who is holding out his hand. "Alma O'Neill told me you were back," he says. He isn't surprised that Henry doesn't quite place him, sees him – rightly – as another of those familiar shadows from his youth and adolescence, someone from the fringes of his solitary world. But Henry is embarrassed by his lapse and the other man is quick to cover.

"I'm Pete Mays, Henry, remember?"

Henry does remember then, a gawky, dreamy, bespectacled boy – his looks have not changed much - who managed to get along with others but was too polite or shy to push his way in and was never asked to join. It never occurred to people to ask him.

He takes the proffered hand. "I remember you. I don't think I've seen you since high school."

Pete blushes and fidgets with the camera case dangling at his side.

Henry's eyes travel to the case. "So that's what you do."

"Not professionally, at least not often. Weddings sometimes. I teach English in the high school."

45

"Well, Professor?" The line in front of them has disappeared. Ricky stands waiting, arms crossed, smirking, mimicking - although he does not see it - his own authority. Like Henry, Pete grew up with the taunts of this bullying man but has outgrown his fear of him.

"Roll of stamps, Ricky, please. Can you put it on the high school tab?" Pete turns to Henry. "Would you care to go for coffee? I can wait for you outside." He looks down at his long, weak feet, notes how they point to Henry's well-formed, competent ones, and then back up at Henry's face. The two disconcerting pairs of eyes meet in speculation.

Henry hides his annoyance. He has not expected this, to be dragged from self-pity by a boy from high school. It would be easier to remain where he is and cultivate his loneliness.

But he says, "Sure. That would be nice. I'll meet you outside," then turns to face his old adversary, who is reaching in the slot for Bella's mail. He pushes it carelessly across the counter.

"So, Henry. I hear you're back to stay this time. Things not so good up there in Sodom, huh?" His grin is sly, his teeth sharp and yellow in the wet mouth. His breath hits Henry's nostrils as he leans across the counter wanting to do damage. But the days for that are long past.

"Things are fine." He can't refrain from asking, "Who told you I was staying?'

"Word gets around. You're the second person to ask me that today. " He is in the middle of snorting in response to Henry's thanks and sputum hits the counter. He wipes it away with his shirt sleeve.

Henry is thinking, this is the world I left.

"What, Henry?" Ricky leans across the counter again and Henry is afraid that this time the spit will hit him. Nevertheless, he stops and looks straight into the other man's eye.

"I said it's so nice to see you again after all these years Ricky."

The fat man is astonished; it isn't until Henry reaches the door and puts his hand upon the knob that Ricky finds words, a word.

Faggot.

As Henry comes down the steps from the post office Pete approaches from the side of the building; the camera is now in his hands, its empty case still hanging at his side. He motions for Henry to follow him and turns back to disappear around the corner from which he has come.

A drainage ditch gurgles behind the building, its stagnant water full of tadpoles. Pete crouches beside the ditch taking pictures, and Henry hunkers down beside him.

"This is how you teachers spend your time."

"When we're not subverting young minds. You manage to fend Ricky off?'

"More or less," Henry replies. "What do you teach?"

"Officially, English and History. He's a bastard. I could have stayed.' Pete looks up and grins. "To protect you, like. But I figured you could handle it. Don't want to squander my authority, do I?"

"Not on me. I can handle Ricky during the day. I wouldn't want to run up against him in a dark alley though."

"That's unlikely. His wife keeps him locked up; besides, he's a coward when he doesn't have ten other bullies to back him up. You don't need to worry about Ricky anymore." He changes the subject. "Another month and this'll be full of mosquito larvae I guess. But it's great now. Remember when we were kids, making tadpole farms?" It isn't the kind of thing Henry remembers but he doesn't say so; he lets Pete recount the memory. "I'd spend all day Saturday carefully making little enclosures –

I even called 'em pastures – for the critters, then I'd come back on Sunday and they would all have turned into frogs and hopped away. I was in complete despair." He laughs again. "I just got this lens. Wanted to try it out. See just how abstract I can make this tadpole farm look."

"It'll be like sperm under a microscope," Henry observes.

"Uh huh, sort of. But it's mostly light and shadow, and then this sort of pattern that I'm interested in." He points to a place where the mud has been spiraled by some turbulence. When the tadpoles swim across and throw their tiny shadows on the mud below, the effect is more artistic than a drainage ditch would suggest.

"It's great," says Pete, sitting back on his haunches. "Just great. Could be anything. You could doctor that picture to be just about anything. Deluge, all consuming fire, or nothing, plain old nothing. The face of the moon. Or just this teensy little tadpole ditch. I have a friend in the forestry service, flies a plane – he takes me up sometimes. Talk about strange, beautiful pictures-" He twists his muddy knees toward Henry, who is trying fastidiously to stay clean, and laughs yet again – to Henry's ear it is a clean, pure tone. Pete gets to his feet, looks down at his pants and shakes his head. "I'm a mess. Good thing I'm a teacher and so respectable or they wouldn't let me in at the Inn. Let's go." He pulls Henry to his feet, and notices as Henry winces. "Did I hurt you?"

"No," Henry says. "It's an old work injury that's been acting up."

"That why you're home?"

"It would be as well if Bella thinks so. "

"I don't suppose she'd take to the idea of you coming home because of her."

"No." He doesn't elaborate. "To tell the truth, my knee didn't seem so bad until I tackled the steps up to the house. I don't see how she does it."

"I don't think she does much anymore," says Pete. "I've been worried - I try to get by there now and again. She won't go to the doctor but I believe old Doc Shumate looks in every so often."

"Still practicing. He must be ancient now."

"Compared to most of his patients he doesn't seem so old. It's an aging population around here you know. Not very many of the young ones stay." He sounds as if he is ancient and looks like a fifteen-year-old as he holds open the door of the Inn for Henry.

The Inn is the oldest building in the valley – early nineteenth century. Its present owner tries to preserve an illusion of yesteryear grandeur and fails because he lacks both money and taste. His business endeavor succeeds strictly on the basis of his good nature and that of his clientelle. The building looks much as it always has in Henry's lifetime, both quaint and tacky, and he finds the combination endearing. It is one of his favorite places in the valley. When he was small Bella brought him here for Sunday dinner, and they feasted upon leather steaks, cardboard potatoes, and canned pears. Anything was better than Bella's cooking and the odd loneliness of their house on the hill. Here there were other families eating their Sunday dinners, the same Sunday dinner that they were eating.

They enter the dining room and Henry's eyes fondly scan the proportions of the room, the graceful choreography of the four center columns, the large fireplace. They find a table by one of the windows that look out over the river and Henry's eyes rest on the vase of cheerful plastic flowers between them. He sets the flowers on an adjoining table.

"This place doesn't change."

"No, says Pete, "I reckon not." He sets his camera on the table and lets the case fall to the floor. "That's why we love it so much." He grins his big awkward grin. He looks like a puppy. A wolfhound puppy, too big for itself, homely and ungainly, a little silly, a little daunting- he might jump on you, knock you down and lick you to death, except that his eyes are full of an un-doglike intelligence. "Well, isn't it?" he is still serene even though he is fingering the camera strap. "It's one of the reasons you've come home – it doesn't change."

The sense of comfortable camaraderie is disturbed. Henry plays with his utensils, sips his coffee, looks out the window. Perhaps he is reading too much into Pete's words. He doesn't know him well enough to be able to tell. "Maybe," he admits at last, and meets the perceptive gaze. "That might be true. Partly true."

A little smile plays on Pete's lips. "Only it isn't true, that this place doesn't change. That's just a, whatdoyacallit – an illusion." He waits, then.

Henry frowns. "Did you bring me here to analyze my motives? I've just come home. Everyone does that. Beyond that, you don't know me well enough to pry."

"I apologize," Pete says, raising one hand in a gesture of peace. " I didn't know I was prying. You know us country boys, we always put our feet in our mouths. I just thought, you know, we might talk, enjoy each other's company, catch up, pretend we used to know each other better than we did. I told you, it's an aging population here in the Kramer Valley."

Henry's face relaxes and he leans back in his chair. "Sorry. I'm sorry. You're right. Besides you, Linda Paisley, and, I reluctantly suppose, Ricky Davies, I wouldn't recognize a single person here. Not of our generation. And Bella's - well, there's Doc Shumate and the odd face here and there. Bella's not exactly part of a large friendly circle."

"No, I know," Pete agrees. "Your mother's a loner. I don't really get that about her, she's so gregarious. But shy deep down, I guess."

"I don't know what it is with her, but then why would I? She's my mother – would you know that sort of thing about your mother?"

"I don't know," Pete says. "She died a long time ago - I barely remember her."

"I'm sorry. I'd forgotten, if I ever knew."

Pete shrugs. "She died a year or so after your father I think. When were you here last? Three years ago?"

"Four."

"That long. I doubt much has changed, to your eyes."

"What about to yours?'

"Not much." Before Pete's courage can fail him he blurts, "I saw you dance last year. In fact, I saw you twice. Two nights in a row." Now that is a surprise.

"My sister Mary Kay went to law school at Columbia – imagine that. I went to her graduation. She knew you and I were in school together, so she took me to see you one night. She was a little hard-put to know what to do with me there. It's the only time I've ever been. She's in Pittsburgh now – big city girl. The next night I got my own ticket and went again. *Songs and Ayres*, your piece was called.

"I liked it. I really did. The only kind of dance I'd ever seen was square dancing – and what they do on Lawrence Welk. Does that count? I don't know anything about it but I liked it a lot. A couple of them were funny – I didn't know dance could be like that. I laughed out loud."

"So that was what I heard," Henry jokes. It falls a little flat.

"Yeah, well. I'm not sophisticated enough to know when to hold it back."

"Neither are New Yorkers."

"I liked the way you used irony – at least I think that's what you were doing – sometimes contrasting the music to the movement. But only sometimes. At other times – well, it was so beautiful I almost cried."

Pete stops. He has gotten too carried away even for a man who doesn't worry about what other people think. He is used to his own shortcomings and knows better than to expect to impress anyone, especially the sophisticated stranger sitting across from him now. But what he can't abide is the thought that his observations might be mistaken for flattery. "I don't express myself very well," he says.

"Could've fooled me."

"I'd like to know. What made you think of dancing to those songs? Even if I'd known how to, I never would have thought of doing that."

Songs and Ayres was Henry's first attempt to set a dance on Early Music; it was the prelude to *Dowland Dances*. His practice piece.

Henry suddenly has a vision of himself twenty-four years earlier, sitting on the floor by the bookshelf from which he has pulled all the music books. He can't even read the words very easily; the musical notation not at all. But it is so beautiful, the long lines rhythmically divided and embellished with those curious markings. And every single one of the books belonged to Max – there was his name in the front of each of them, Henry did know enough to recognize that, the most important thing of all.

"My father," Henry says.

"What?" The silence has gone on for so long that Pete has forgotten his own question.

"You asked what made me think of dancing to those songs. It was my father."

They leave the Inn and part company by the road. Henry waits until Pete has started his car then turns and walks in the opposite direction. He has a visit to make.

Away from his mother's house the numbing inertia is less powerful, and Linda Paisley's house isn't far from the Inn. He limps up the twisting alley, careful to avoid the potholes, and leans against the wire fence across the street from the modest green dwelling. He is unaware of Linda watching him from her second story bedroom window.

She has a comfortable chair by that window and often sits there, because in a household consisting of herself, her fourteen year old daughter, and the memory of her dead brother, it is the one place that feels like her own. She keeps books and magazines stacked on the floor beside the chair and often reads there, or sews, but at the moment she is doing neither. She has been staring out the window and past the inn, watching the water play down the rocks of the falls. She sees Pete and Henry enter the inn. She sees them come out forty-five minutes later, stand by the side of the road, say their good-byes. She knows Henry well enough, even now, to see his distraction, and knows from the direction in which his head keeps tilting what the likely cause is. She watches him come up the alley and resists the anxiety she feels as she notices his limp. When he stops in front of her house and leans into the fence opposite, her body relaxes in its shared relief at the weight taken from whatever joint or muscle is giving him trouble.

She never remembers how beautiful he is; like the pain of childbirth, his beauty is something you think you can never forget, and then you do. It has been years since she has seen him and he has changed very little. The refinements of age have modified the sense of sadness lent his gray eyes by their downward slope. His cheekbones, now a little more prominent, support the sockets in such a way that sadness is too simple a word to describe the impression of the eyes. His back is ramrod straight, the long limbs perfectly controlled, even when he's limping. And it is mostly that – his carriage – which makes him breathtaking. He has always carried himself that way, as if to reject any suggestion of slovenliness or vulnerability, but the posture itself makes him vulnerable; he is too self-contained. It was a characteristic he had shared with her brother Jack, but to such different effect. There was nothing vulnerable about Jack, yet he is the one who is dead.

When Henry stands as he does now, lost to the world in his own thoughts, there is always that odd look of surprise as though he cannot believe his own rage or indecision. Linda is sure it is the latter and so she pushes the screen aside and leans out the window.

"Enough reverie, Henry. Come on in now!" She shouts much as she would have thirteen years earlier, and he obeys as he did then. He squints up at her and limps toward the front steps. She leaps down the stairs and reaches the door before he does, pushing the screen door open; it lacks a spring and crashes into the wall in much the same way that she crashes into him, except that she envelopes him in her large embrace while the door slaps helplessly against the siding. She shepherds him inside and tries to make him sit, but he resists her.

"Wait, wait." He takes her two arms above the elbow so that he can hold her away from himself and look at her, framed by the unchanged room that she filled long ago with her collection of ugly dolls. He has never understood why she keeps them, why she has them in the first place. But that isn't what he is thinking about. He is wondering the same thing she is: why do they greet each other after all these years as though they had seen each other only yesterday?

"But your leg. You should sit. What's wrong with it?"

"I've been sitting for a week now. Don't worry, it's just a dancer's plague. It will heal." He kisses her on both cheeks and lets her draw him to the sofa. His little bundle of mail has fallen to the floor, and Linda bends to retrieve it and throws it on the coffee table. She pushes him down on the sofa then crosses her arms and studies him while he gazes at her, resigned to her attention.

"Well it had better. You were looking awful serious out there, leaning on my fence. I heard you were here."

"I was feeling serious, leaning on your fence. I have so many amends to make. I never even wrote to you when Jack died." Linda grows very still. "I don't have a good excuse – it was cowardice, pure and simple. Could you please sit down, and let me try to talk? If I don't say as much as I can now, I may lose my nerve again and never get it back." She does as he asks, in the chair directly opposite the one he occupies.

"It was so long ago, Henry." Her voice is quiet, almost a whisper.

"I was in my final year at Juilliard, and I kept getting messages from other students living on the hall saying you'd called. I already knew he'd been killed though – for all my irresponsibility, the one thing I have done all these years is telephone Bella once a week. She told me, in her sprightly by-the-way fashion. I didn't want to talk to you. I didn't know what I could say. First I left Deep River for Juilliard and abandoned Jack to take all the abuse, then I managed a 4F and he didn't. I was supposed to tell you I was *sorry?* Even I wasn't capable of such hypocrisy. It was far worse than that though, because I didn't feel anything. Not a thing, Linda, do you understand? Jack became a part of my past I didn't need to think about anymore – and you along with him. In fact, it was that same month that I got my first write-up in the *Times* - my big *entré.* I just went on, dancing my merry way. No, don't interrupt me. I'm only back here now because my sins seem to be finally catching up with me. Witness the limp – and some other things I don't need to burden you with. I'm going to try and atone by taking care of Bella. She's very ill, although she won't admit it. I just want you to know – I don't think I have feelings, and my ethical sense is also somewhat shaky. Until recently at least, my ambition was the only intact emotional tool I possessed. I deserve to have you slap me across the face or beat me to a pulp, whatever you like. That's why I came."

She has an urge to laugh hysterically but resists it. She resists also the impulses that follow – first to chide him for his self-pity, then for his misjudgment, then to indulge in irony of a sophomoric type. At last she settles for giving him a scrap of information he doesn't have. "Jack didn't try to get a deferment."

He stares. "That's not true. We talked about what we'd do."

"He didn't have your dedication to a particular endeavor, Henry. His talent was high school football. He didn't approve of the war, but he liked the idea of being a soldier. He came to believe that people like him – who didn't approve of the war – were the ones who *should* go, because they had the right idea about it all and would come up with better solutions. It had nothing to do with you, so you can stop beating yourself over the head about Jack at least. In addition, I don't believe you about your lack of feeling, but please don't feel you need to set me straight. I haven't seen you in ten years; let me make you some coffee."

"Please, no. I've just spent half the morning drinking coffee. First at home, then with Pete Mays."

She notices the word, home. "Pete Mays. He's a dear man, but I've observed that he does drink a lot of coffee."

"Jack and I never really knew him. He was at high school when we were, but a year behind or ahead I think. I don't remember classes with him."

" He was the year behind you. I doubt either you or Jack would have noticed him back then."

"You like him though."

"I go out with him sometimes. Everyone likes Pete, with the possible exception of Ricky Davies, who doesn't like anyone. Pete is one of those rare people who gets better and better, the older he is. He can't seem to do enough for others, and he's not even annoying about it."

"I think he wanted to pry into my secrets."

"Do you have secrets? He might have been trying to pry," she says, "but it would have been meant as a way for you to purge your rotten soul, whereas if it had been me I would just be hankering to sate my insatiable curiosity. Ricky Davies is spreading a rumor that New York has exiled you."

She reads his answering silence. "Panic attack?"

"What do you mean?"

"I mean you look like someone who's running away."

Before he can think, he reaches out to grasp her wrist in a way that hurts her; when he realizes what he is doing he lets go. Shocked, she loses her balance and tumbles forward toward him. He catches her and helps her right herself, but his anger freezes the air between them.

"You don't know what you're talking about," he tells her. She remembers this look of his, and the tone - a haughtiness fashioned for hiding behind. She tries to recapture his hand, but he has pulled far away from her, into the corner of the sofa.

She stares at him, and he avoids her eyes until she resumes her seat opposite the sofa.

"I wonder when was the last time you confided in anyone," she says while he is engrossed in a study of one of her atrocious dolls. "Thirteen years ago, in this house? Forgive me, Henry, if I'm making assumptions, but it occurs to me that you came back here to find someone to confide in. You could have gone somewhere else: Jack isn't here anymore, you and I've lost touch, and you've never been close to your mother. Surely someone as influential as you are becoming has many friends." She hesitates, then adds, "You must be very tired."

After a moment, he shifts so that he is not facing quite so much away from her. "You are only partly right," he says. "I am a little tired, it's true - I've worked hard these past years– and I need to work up my nerve to have surgery on this knee. Silly, isn't it? The thought of an operation scares me. And I did think of going somewhere else, and no, I don't confide in anyone. It makes me feel vulnerable." He finally looks straight at her. "*You* make me feel vulnerable."

"Well, God knows why."

"About a month ago, a colleague –someone I'd had a close friendship with a few years ago – killed himself. Our relationship was complicated, or maybe it just felt complicated – he had a drug problem and it interfered with his work. I'd made a principal role for him in my new dance, and then the artistic director fired him. He overdosed that night."

"That wasn't your fault," Linda protests.

"That's not for you to say." She knows he is right. "Oh, it wasn't *all* my fault, I know that, but I played a part – my coldness did. It was the same as when Jack died - don't feel anything. When Hector fired Ray, I was relieved, even though I'd made that part for him. And then that night, he died, and it was like having an invisible hand push my relief to its utmost extreme. I went to identify the body. Talk about cold. And then I went home and threw up. After that, of all things, I called Bella."

Those two things – throwing up and calling Bella, prove you have feelings."

"No." He is adamant. "How your body reacts has nothing to do with feelings."

"And calling Bella was your body reacting?"

"Why not? The infantile instinct for the maternal bosom. My father is the parent I've actually always wanted, but then – like so many others – he's dead. Bella is as close as I can get to him, but I don't feel anything for her either, except revulsion, my version of pity, but she's ill and I'm her son. It must have been Dr. Roberts who's told everyone I'm here. "

"His nurse, more likely – she's been known to abuse patient confidentiality before. You're hard on your mother, Henry. She's done her best all these years – it's not easy to raise a child alone."

"No, I know it's not, but on the other hand, you don't know her very well. The one thing I can thank her for I suppose is dragging me along to that school of hers.

Even that seems a mixed blessing."

"You don't mean that."

He shrugs and pulls himself to his feet. "No, probably not. But it was Max who insisted on the dance school, did I ever tell you? So I actually own the dream – if it is a dream – to him."

"Did Bella tell you that?" Linda asks.

" More or less; and I pieced it together, from old financial records and things Bella has said. I don't think she's ever had an energetic bone in her body. I wonder what she seemed like to Max when he first met her. Why are you looking at me that way?"

"Because it strikes me that you have convinced yourself you know Max far better than Bella, yet you can't possibly remember much about him. You were five when he died."

"I remember him," Henry responds curtly. "Besides, there are all his books. I know him through those."

Linda sighs and changes the subject.

A car door slams, there is a murmur of voices, laughter, and then someone is running up the front steps. A tall girl in a bathing suit enters and stops short when she sees Henry.

"You remember Henry Oliver, Ruthie," Linda says as she puts her arms around the girl and kisses her hair.

"Sort of." And to him, "Hi."

Ruthie looks like Jack. She looks like her mother too, except that in Ruthie and Jack the identical features were assembled to conform to a conventional standard of handsome looks. Big boned and smooth, graceful and slim, with a mass of unruly black curls framing her regular features, Ruthie would outshine her mother physically in the eyes of almost any judge, but not in Henry's eyes. He had adored Jack, and thinks Ruthie is very fine, but he has always loved the riotous abandon with which Linda's attributes had been arranged. A sort of beneficent energy is how he thinks of it, a bit like a cubist painting, threatening to reorganize the spiritual environment. Others think of her as homely.

He holds out his hand to the girl, and when she crosses the room to take it he levers her closer so that he can kiss her cheek. He realizes he makes her self-conscious and wants not to.

"I'll put those towels in the basement," she mumbles shyly and disappears into the kitchen.

"You're the only celebrity Ruthie knows."

"She's lovely," Henry says.

"Yes. Like Jack, you're thinking."

"And like you."

Linda rolls her eyes. "If only I could look like that. Or be as smart."

"I should go," Henry says. As he turns, his eyes linger on the closed door beside the steps leading to the second floor. Linda notices.

"Go in, if you like," she says quietly. "I've never done anything about his things. I'll be in the kitchen making lunch. Come say good-bye to me before you go."

He lays his hand on her arm, and she looks down at the long fingers. "Did your parents at least come to the funeral?" he asks her softly.

"Daddy did. Mama had a stroke when they gave her the news and was in the hospital."

"Jesus, Linda…"

She shakes her head. "Don't say any more. It's a long time ago, isn't it? They're all gone now. Go on in."

She keeps the room clean. There is no dust, only an unused smell. The shaft of sunlight is making its way slowly across the bed.

Jack had been particular about his room – the neutral color of the walls, the style of furniture. He liked things to be modern and masculine, and then he cluttered the clean surfaces with objects: trophies from sports, little boxes, pictures of his sister and niece, of himself, of Henry. Henry picks up the one of Jack and him together at age sixteen, chests bare, arms around each others' shoulders, big grins on their faces. Henry remembers the day it was taken. They had been swimming below the falls and Linda had snapped it on their return.

Linda had practically raised Jack, not because their parents were dead but because they had disowned both children, one at a time, for reasons of respectability: Ruthie's out-of-wedlock birth and Jack's loyalty to her, later compounded by the scandal involving Henry. The scandal. In Linda's newly middle class family, respectability had been the primary virtue, although that must have changed with Jack's death. Henry puts the picture back on the dresser and sits down on the bed.

It seems so insignificant now, in a way, Ricky Davies' sneaking and spying, and the furor over their being caught like that together, out on the Island. It didn't matter anymore. He and Jack had moved off in different directions but both of them into bigger worlds than Deep River. At the time, it had felt like an earthquake. It was the time before the earthquake that comes into Henry's mind now, as he sits on Jack's bed, his nose unconsciously seeking and failing to discover a lingering scent of the one person he had ever truly been close to. They had not parted amicably, and it was Henry's fault – he was the betrayer, taking up his scholarship at Juilliard without a backward glance while Jack was caught in the old abhorred machinery. Except that Linda had just told him differently.

He shuts the door quietly and leaves the house, forgetting to tell Linda goodbye.

3. ENCOUNTERS AND NEGOTIATIONS

Driving home later in the day, Pete thinks about high school. It is Henry who has put him on this track, and sheers him away from the now-amusing memory of how heavily his own awkwardness had weighed upon him then. He thinks instead of his first glimpse of Henry and his friend Jack. It would have been impossible not to notice them, they so decidedly did not fit in and so obviously didn't care. As he stepped down from the school bus on the first day and struggled to keep from tripping on the bus's steep step, he saw Henry, long-limbed and austere, leaning against the big elm by the schoolyard gate. He kept pushing back the straight black hair that threatened to hide his eyes while he listened to something Jack was saying. Jack was much more strongly built but only slightly taller, with skin like bronze next to Henry's alabaster. The contrast was dazzling. Jack leaned slightly toward Henry with his arms crossed and a bemused smile on his lips as he spoke to his friend. Henry shrugged and replied, and they both laughed. Pete saw two things: that they liked each other and that there was a sort of tenderness between them. Their laughter excluded everyone else.

By two years later, when Ricky Davies and his pals followed them out onto the Island, Pete had matured enough to realize that their relationship was far more complicated than the one he thought he envied. He tried, ineffectually it seemed, to deflect the more horrified of his schoolmates' reactions to the scandalous gossip that ensued. The only thing that had come of his effort was an understanding that if he wanted to be listened to, there were certain obstacles of his own that he had better overcome.

The picture of Henry and Jack under the elm remained with him, and over the years he sometimes drew it forth to contemplate. Even at fifteen, standing in the schoolyard, Henry Oliver had "elsewhere" written all over him. In spite of that, Pete had always known that Henry was as tied to the valley as he was. The past is an integument as congenital as skin, and the flaying of one as fatal as that of the other. That day Henry had been holding onto the elm tree, and Pete remembered his hand against the bark, gentle and taut at the same time, as though he feared too rough a touch would harm the tree to which he clung. Now he is back, the exile returned. But the question is the same for everyone: where is the place of exile, and where of belonging? How does one tell them apart?

Roy's tattered Bible lies next to the grinding stone on the workbench that runs down the north side of his house. Pete picks it up and calls Roy's name.

"I'm here," Roy calls back, and a moment later exits the second of his two cellars holding a pair of mason jars. His famous strawberry jam. He sets the jars on the bench and limps toward the house. "I'll put us on some water to boil. You set there on the porch."

Pete hands him the book and watches him go, in his mind matching this old man's limp to that of the man he had left a few hours earlier. He settles into the less comfortable chair before Roy has a chance to make him take the other one, and watches the clouds through the leaves. It might rain tonight, he thinks. Roy returns with two cups of strong boiled tea and without protest sits down on the good chair. Something is wrong.

"What's on your mind, Roy?"

There is a long silence, through which Pete waits patiently. Just before he gives up, Roy replies. "Family things." Pete knows a little about Roy's family.

After a few more minutes, Roy speaks again. "I'm going to be away for awhile. Would you mind keeping an eye out?"

"Of course I'll keep an eye out. Is it Sarah?" Sarah is the love-child of Roy's sister Mae, who had died when she was born. Roy had raised her and doted on her, but she had "run off with the hippies," people said, ten years earlier. There is a rumor that she isn't quite right. Every year or two, Roy receives some word of her and goes off in search. In all that time, he has found her twice and never succeeded in bringing her home. He says nothing of her state of mind, or of his own. Pete doesn't remember her. He has heard that she is unusually beautiful, promiscuous, and completely unlike Roy, whom she calls "Daddy Roy."

"Hmm. Someone's seen her. Mimsy Bradshaw's brother, over in Staunton. I'd better go see if it's true. I'll get the early train in Kramer tomorrow – put me in Staunton around three."

"It's Sunday tomorrow, Roy – I could drive you over. It wouldn't take nearly as long."

Roy's eyes grow bright, and Pete looks away, not wanting to embarrass him.

"I thank you kindly, Mr. Pete, but this is family business – I'd best go alone. And anyway, if you went with me, who'd keep the thieves out of my jam? Now, distract me a little - tell me your doings."

"I saw Henry Oliver this morning – Max's son. He's come back."

Roy's eyes narrow in interest. "That so."

"Seems he's had some setbacks recently – an injury, some problems in New York, and now his mother's pretty sick. He says he's going to stay awhile."

"That so," Roy says again. "Well, his mother needs someone."

"Why did you say she took against you, Roy? Back after Max died?" Roy stares off into space, and Pete knows he's gone back to that time. "What happened, back then?" Pete asks.

Roy is working at something in his mind, and Pete thinks he might almost be about to tell him what happened in those days, but instead he says, "Come help me with the jam."

Pete follows him into the 12 by 15 foot room that serves as bedroom, living room, bathroom and kitchen. It is sweltering, because the woodstove has been going all day while Roy makes his famous strawberry jam. "Forty-three jars this year," Roy mumbles, but Pete is thinking of the coincidence that not two hours earlier he was remembering the big kettle of jam his brother had pulled down on himself. The jars, forty-three minus the two sitting out on the workbench, are lined up in rows on the bed.

"Well, you're going to make a lot of people happy," Pete says as he picks up four jars and starts for the door. Roy gives most of it away.

After they have moved about half of the jam to the cellar built into the hillside behind the house, Roy stops in the doorway, blocking Pete's way. "Ms. Bella and

I had a disagreement about something," Roy says. "I still don't know who was right. It's bothered me all these years. Her too, I reckon."

"You want to talk about it?"

"I do, yes. But I don't know that I have a right to, you see."

Pete doesn't press. After they have delivered the last of the jam to the cellar, except for the two jars Roy gives him, Pete lingers a minute longer. "I'll be up at the house all night if you want to talk to me, Roy, and I'll drive you to the train in the morning. I'm a close-mouthed person, you know. Any secret would be safe with me."

As he walks away Pete wonders whether it's his curiosity or his helpfulness that has the upper hand just now. Roy watches him go with relief for once. He's got enough on his mind with Sarah; he doesn't need to be dodging Pete's persistent concern. All the same, he'd like to see for himself what Max's son has turned out to be like, as a human being.

Henry has been gone a long time and Bella is peevish. The morning has become noon and now afternoon, and she hasn't eaten her lunch. She is always hungry, really, thanks to the perpetual gnawing. When she eats the way she used to everything goes haywire, but

75

she can't not eat. It isn't that she is losing weight that is alarming but that it seems to be falling off of her in ten-pound lots. So she is careful even though she disapproves of being careful, and she waits to eat with Henry because, unlike her, he is watchful of both their diets; he seems to know about nutrition. She has stopped telling herself that they are two independent people and she has neither need of nor right to him. He makes her eat slowly, and she suffers less later. He reads the alarm in her eyes and says something indirectly soothing. And best of all, he keeps everything spotless.

At last tired of waiting, she opens a can of soup and is spooning it out of the saucepan and into a bowl when she hears the front door open.

"Henry?" Her voice sounds scratchy and grating, even to her.

A moment later Henry appears in the doorway. He hesitates a moment before walking forward and throwing the mail on the table. He pulls out the other chair and sits. How does he always manage to sit so straight? The first thing she wants to do when she's off her feet is slouch, even in these old uncomfortable ladderbacks.

"Soup?"

He shakes his head and lies. "I ate at the Paisleys." It slips out, "The Paisleys," as though Jack were still there rounding out the household. Surprisingly, Bella holds her tongue on that one.

"I wondered where you were," she says instead and is unable to keep a tiny edge of complaint out of her voice. To modify it, she asks, "And how is Linda Paisley?"

"Fine."

"Pretty girl, her daughter. She looks like your friend Jack." It pleases her to see she has surprised him.

"I had coffee with Pete Mays," Henry tells her.

She can't help it – the old habit is too deeply engrained. "My surrogate son. Not as handsome or as celebrated as the real thing, but ready to hand."

Henry stiffens. "I'm home. Isn't that enough for now?"

She shrugs, but there is a faint, trouble-making smile on her lips. "Sure."

When Bella goes up to take a nap she looks out the window and sees Henry sitting on the wall. What book is it this time? Not Petrarch. One of the Classical Library books. She squints. Red. Latin. She had once read Latin and Greek both – they hardly teach either in the schools in this country whereas the classics had been the foundation of her education. How envious Max had been of that. Sometimes she thinks it is a pity that American children are so ill-taught and at other times she wonders what possible difference it makes. They are dead languages, after all. She should remind Henry to take the books when he returns to New York. She watches as he lays the book on the wall and starts up the hill, disappearing shortly into the trees. She knows where he is heading – she followed him once, and got away with it. He always goes – has always gone - to that odd little flat place with the moss-covered rocks. Trillium blooms up there in the spring, an otherworldly flower. The red dust jacket of the book stands out brightly against the stone. Something moves. Fascinated, she sees a chipmunk dart out of a crevice and inspect the book. Three feet away, a black snake emerges, sizes up its quarry and begins its slow glide. A kind of panic activates Bella. She pushes open the window and shouts. The chipmunk only looks up, perfectly aware that she is too far away to pose a danger. The snake slithers, coils. Bella grabs the first thing her hand reaches – a small Meissen bird - and throws. The bird crashes aptly into the wall, the chipmunk disappears into a hole, and an instant later the tail of the snake has merged with the dirt around the rhizomes of the irises growing there. It's as though the brutal little scenario never happened. Her gaze travels up the hillside to where Henry has emerged from his sanctuary to see what the ruckus was. He stands a moment and then disappears again. Bella begins to weep and stumbles like an old woman to her bed.

When Max died, Roy Bright came to the house. They didn't know each other very well. He was part of Max's other life. She had always thought he seemed nice, and when he called her "Ms. Oliver," she asked him to call her Bella. He could only manage "Ms. Bella," but kindly explained to her the southern traditions he found so difficult to shake.

He got there before the police did. It was in February and had been either raining or snowing off and on all day, so that the roads were a mess, but still he had driven up there from his home in the hollow where there was the colored community, that's what they called it back then. She had just put Henry to bed and knew Max would be quite late if he came at all, so she was surprised when she heard the footsteps on the porch. She assumed it was Max and ran to the door. Even after the almost ten years of their marriage she still ran to the door, as if early-courtship behavior could obliterate the interim infidelities. Roy took off his hat and asked if he could come in.

She knew something was wrong, because he didn't bother to say pleasant things and also because he led her into the living room, poked the fire, then sat down opposite her before she could invite him to. It couldn't have been more than two minutes between when he walked in the door and when he started to speak, but it seemed like a length of time that could encompass her marriage to Max. Once he started to tell her though, he was careful not to drag it out.

"Something bad's happened, Ms. Bella. Max is dead – shot by a man down at Edgewater. They're putting it about that it was a legal dispute – the man who did it was a company tenant – but I'm going to tell you the truth, because you'd suspect it anyway, that it was over a woman. The police will tell you the other story, but I thought you'd want to know."

And he was right. In not pretending to protect her from the truth, Roy was telling her that he too knew the real Max, the charming, self-absorbed and complicated man - the cold and hypocritical thief of her self-confidence, whom she had loved. He was trying to say that if she wanted someone to talk to that he would keep her confidence. He told her the killer was an ordinary meek man, sorry about the whole business. A plea bargain would mean the affair could be hushed up.

Henry heard their voices and appeared on the landing, and she lit a cigarette as Roy picked him up and carried him down to sit with them. She smoked and watched, as Roy told Henry that Max was gone, but not of course the truth of what had happened. Henry wept and Roy coaxed him into calmness, until Henry went to the bookshelf and brought over one of the books he couldn't yet read, to show Roy Max's name on the flyleaf. Then, in her mind, the pendulum swung from a belief that now everything would repair itself and, once the grief was past, be clean and new, to a conviction that for Henry's sake the old half-truths and white lies must never be abandoned. He no longer had a father; she must insure that he had an image of a father.

Not long after, the police came and conveyed to her their deep sorrow at the tragedy. Such a loss to the community.

When Henry comes down from the hillside and retrieves his book from where he abandoned it on the wall, he spies the delicately painted head of the Meissen bird nearby and picks it up. Puzzled by its sudden appearance, he carries it inside and sets it on the kitchen table next to the mail. There is a letter for him.

He carries it upstairs, peeks into Bella's room to find her lying on the bed with her back to the door, and passes on, thinking he will go to his own room, but his eye lights on the door to the attic stairs when he passes it, he changes his mind, opens the door and ascends.

Long ago, when Max brought Bella home and hoped to make her happy, he transformed the barren third floor into a practice room for her, a retreat from the sooty drabness of the valley. A place where she could remind herself that she was a dancer, an artist, and an Englishwoman.

He pushes open the door at the top of the narrow stairs and lets his eye follow the contours of the room. It is musty and airless now with lack of use, the second such room Henry has entered that day. The floor space is large, running the length and width of the house, but on the front its use is limited by the slant of the roof-line. Mirrors, barricaded by a portable barre, line the opposite wall. A spinet piano, the only kind to be gotten up those narrow steps, faces him against the far wall. He notices a faint smell of damp and turns on the light to look. It is easy to spot: the worst place is high on the wall to the left of the piano – a dark, fungus-encrusted place. But it isn't the only one. He recalls the holes in the roofline that he had been able to see from the post office. He sits down in the shabby Victorian rocker beside the piano and turns it toward the dirty window, then rocks a little. It has been ages since he was in here. It had long ago become the place for putting the boxes of old bank records and papers that no one knew what to do with; they were stacked in all three corners. Yet darkened paintings still adorn the once-white walls: coastal Cornwall, Iona, and New Forest. He remembers looking through books of pictures of Britain; remembers being told about these paintings. Over the window someone, it must have been Max, had painted a Greek inscription. Henry knows what it means because he has read his father's Herodotus and is also aware that T.E.Lawrence had once carved the same inscription over his cottage door: *doesn't care*. Looking at it, Henry has to smile. It suits Bella.

The letter is lying in his lap, the address in its familiar

handwriting glaring up at him. Wearily, he sticks his index finger under the unpasted corner, breaks the envelope along the crease, extracts and unfolds the two pages.

Thursday, June 14th, 1979.

Henry,

What am I doing writing you a letter, for God's sake? You did jot down a phone number (are there actually telephone lines in those parts?), but somehow I fear to use it. This is to let you know that the premiere is 12 days away (probably 6 by the time this reaches you) and your absence is noticed by one and all. I checked: there's an airport only 40 miles from you. Can't you at least fly back for a day or two, to boost morale and attend your own triumph? The expense would be paid of course. It would be more effective to call, I know – it's much easier for you to greet this epistle with silence. I think I may be working up to calling.

As you requested, Enrico will dance Ray's part opening night, and then share it with Robert for the rest of the City Center season. Stanton is busy being you. They are all up to your standard, don't worry. The lighting guys have had some questions, which I've done my best to answer authoritatively. It would be really nice if you were here to back me up.

About everything else, the less said the better I'm sure you'll agree.

Au revoir,

HG

Henry lets the letter drift to the floor and leans his head back against the wooden ridge at the top of the rocker. He hopes Hector won't call – can't imagine what they might say to each other any more than he can imagine going back to New York for the opening. It was just eight days ago that he had left but it seemed like a year. In fact, it is his old nightmare come true: that he *has* been here forever and that it's his New York life that is the dream. He had been so dogged about dancing in spite of his knee; now he can't imagine why. His mind works differently here; he hardly thinks about dancing at all, much less imagines the musical structure of a dance. He thinks about Bella – worries about her, actually – and about washing the dishes, running the vacuum, cooking a meal that she can keep down. When he remembers anything, it's the very distant past, the part of his life over which his work has been such a reliable veil, a sort of altar to Max. Until now. Now he remembers Jack, not in a general way but in small details: a certain angle of his head when he had something funny to say, his hand unbuttoning his top button, tying his shoe – those kinds of inconsequential things. He remembers the little girls, all shapes and sizes, in his mother's classes. He remembers how it felt, getting his arms and hands just right and straining that first day to see around the children in front of him. He remembers Max.

Not much about Max though. Hardly anything. He has one memory, a time when Max took him to visit an old German man, another chemist at the plant, who lived with his grown daughter in a house with a gazebo beside the road leading to the Kramer bridge. The daughter was overweight, smelled of onions and played the piano. They had tea and hard German cookies; Max and the man talked while Henry and the girl sat awkwardly on the piano bench. He remembers all of that, and he remembers the drive home when Max explained in grotesque terms how the German chemist and his daughter came to live here because they were Jewish. He only understood the explanation much later, but he remembers the day clearly. It is the one distinct memory he has of Max.

He has no such memories of Bella. When he realizes that she is excluded from this mental excursion into the past, he tries to dredge something up and fails. This, he acknowledges, is peculiar. Yet he thinks of her constantly in the present – he is worried sick, in fact, and not sure if there is something he should be doing.

When he opens his eyes, the afternoon sun has dropped behind a hill and the room is practically dark although outdoors there is still daylight. He shuffles toward the stairs while his eyes gradually adjust to an awareness of the shadowy forms around him. His knee is quite stiff again and his back a little achy from his body's effort to compensate.

Bella is as he left her, lying on her side with her back to the door. This time, he tiptoes into her room, close enough to hear her lightly troubled breathing. He doesn't want to wake her – he will start dinner uninterrupted and then see if she's stirred.

He has thawed a chicken and after he gets it into the oven he wanders over to the cabinet where Bella keeps her sherry. He's not much of a drinker but is beginning to understand the logic behind the habit. He would have a glass of decent wine now if one were offered. But sherry? He pulls out the cork and sniffs, pours a little in a cup, tastes, grimaces and pours it in the sink. He will have to find some other way to deal with this unfamiliar restlessness. Upstairs, he hears the creaking of floorboards, a scrape, and something that might be a cry. He rushes through the hall and up the stairs.

Bella has slipped on the silly little rug in the bathroom and hit her head.

"I'm fine. I'm fine," she protests," as he prods. There is a little blood glimmering in the hair over her left ear. Carefully he lifts her and carries her back to the bed. He has to shove the books, magazines, and clothes aside to lay her down. She groans, half in pain and half in annoyance. Henry reaches for the phone beside the bed, pulls the list of numbers out from under it, finds Doc Roberts' and dials. "What are you doing?" she asks, knowing perfectly well.

Doc Roberts is home having his dinner. Henry returns the mouthpiece to its cradle. "He'll be here in fifteen minutes."

"I wish you hadn't called him," Bella says, but her voice lacks conviction and her eyes are unaccusing.

"I should have called him the day I got back," Henry replies. "Does anything hurt?"

"Only where I bumped my head. I didn't break anything if that's what you're worried about." She grimaces.

"We'll see what he says. You should let him look you over anyway, run some tests. When was the last time you saw him?"

Bella doesn't reply, which is answer enough. "Bring me some sherry," she says, and he refuses.

Doc Roberts has been one of only a handful of physicians in the valley since Henry can remember. He is seventy now, and afraid to retire because there is no one to replace him. The little hospital in Kramer is shrinking, likely to be incorporated into the city medical center an hour away. He will stall the process for as long as possible, as one by one his old patients die off. Now Bella is among their number.

Henry answers the door.

"Well, Henry, when was the last time I saw you?" He answers his own question as they shake hands. "Thirteen, fourteen years ago now. I hear things have gone well for you. It's good to see you."

"And you, Sir. Bella's upstairs." The doctor follows him up and makes note of the limp, which, in his preoccupation with Bella, Henry neglects to hide.

"Well, Bella. Forced to see me at last. It's a good thing your son is here." He bends over her and gently pulls up her eyelid, then sits on the edge of the bed. They have known each other a long time. In spite of Bella's aversion to doctors, they are friends.

"That's right, James. I wouldn't be caught dead calling you or any other doctor for that matter. You only know how to make things worse, with all your poking and prodding. So you can thank people like Henry for your bread and butter."

The doctor turns toward Henry, who is standing in the doorway. "Thank you, Henry. Now leave me alone with this ornery woman, will you?"

"I'll go take the chicken out of the oven," Henry says.

As he goes downstairs he hears their voices, and their familiarity with each other is obvious even though he can't hear what they say. He doesn't have that sort of casual rapport with Bella. He had wanted to take her hand, up there, while they were waiting for Doc Roberts. He hadn't been able to.

He has put the food out on the counter and is debating whether or not to let it cool before he puts it in the refrigerator when Doc Roberts joins him. He sets his bag on the floor and leaned against the sink.

"As far as hitting her head goes, it's not too bad – I'm more worried about her other symptoms and the fact she fell in the first place. She's lost a lot of weight, has a lot of bruising, not all of it from this evening. She says she's always tired. Can you bring her to the hospital tomorrow morning? I'd like to keep her overnight and run tests. Don't worry – I've demanded and received her grudging agreement so your head is safe for now. Promised her two lollipops instead of the usual one. I noticed your limping. Want me to take a look?"

Henry shakes his head. "I already know what I need to do – I just keep putting it off. It's my knee."

"Surgery?"

"Yes. I've just been too busy. It's been worse, actually, since I got here."

"Well, you're not using it as much – it stiffens up. Could be a little psychological too, don't you think?

Judging from the infrequency of your visits, I'd guess it's stressful being here."

Henry laughs. "No more than being in New York. Just different." He doesn't want to talk about himself. "What time should we be there?"

"Eight o'clock. Remember where my office is, in the old wing? Bring her there – I'll deal with the red tape."

In the morning he leaves her with Doc Roberts and is again conscious, overhearing their banter, of a twinge of regret that his mother is more comfortable with the doctor, even though she distrusts doctors.

He drives up the hill to the old dance school and parks in one of the three spaces in front of the neglected building. Dandelions and burdock push through the broken asphalt, and from where he sits in his car, in spite of the dense summer foliage, Henry can see where the mountain across the river has been cut away for coal. The building itself is a low, nondescript place with room for two other businesses, but he sees no signs of life in any of them. Off to the right is a service station; someone looks out the window. Henry sits in the car and stares at the place where he got his start, and where Bella's career ended. What *had* been her dreams, he wonders. She must have had them, once. He realizes he isn't even sure when she stopped teaching.

She used to keep a key in a little hole between the

cinderblock base and the doorframe – the obvious hiding place, but no one had ever disturbed it. Almost unconsciously, he seeks it, removing the pebble and sticking his index finger in – the key is still there.

He nearly chokes on the smell of mildew when he opens the door. He reaches for the light switch and a hazy yellow light floods the room, lingers in the cloudy glass of the mirrors. He walks to the window and pulls the string to raise the Venetian blind. It doesn't help much. Coal dust mixed with rainwater renders the glass practically opaque. He wanders to the back, where there is a small bathroom and kitchenette. He tries everything: the toilet flushes, the water runs, the little two-burner electric stove gets hot. He pushes the switch on the hot water heater and that too rumbles into operation. There are still cleaning supplies in the narrow closet. He doesn't know why, but he cleans with a vengeance, finishing with the front window. While he is cleaning the outside, the man from the service station wanders over.

"About to open the place?" His friendliness has a suspicious edge.

"Maybe," Henry says, wiping away the suds and grime that coat the glass..

"What sort of business?"

Henry dips the rag in the bucket and scrubs. "It's a dance school."

The man laughs. "I hear that's what it used to be – ten, fifteen years ago. I wasn't here then. People stopped sending their kids to her, is what I heard – they said she was always a little off but especially after her son left. He's some kind of dance star in New York City, never comes to see her. Her husband used to run the plant, everybody liked him but he died tragically. Nice man, they say. Cared about people."

"I'm her son," Henry says curtly. He picks up the bucket, wants to get away somewhere. His chest is tight. "Excuse me." He brushes past the man, goes inside and locks the door.

The room is spotless now, down to the keys on the old out-of-tune piano and the turntable on the little record player. He puts his finger under the arm to see if there is a needle. Yes. From the stack of a dozen records, he chooses Chopin and puts it on, listens to the scratching sound preceding the first polonaise, then closes his eyes and attempts to imagine himself inside the music. He can't. He wants to; if only he could lose himself to it, discover its emotional core and be overtaken by it. He can't. He can't. He grits his teeth, executes a series of angry jetés entrelacés, feels his knee falter, and kicks the arm away from the record, breaking it. Still the record turns. In one last effort at what to him is sanity, he turns it off and sits down on the piano bench, runs his fingers over the keys then settles into a Bach Invention, one of the only things he can play from memory. The instrument is so out of tune that it sounds like a clown's toy piano. He forces himself through the Invention just to see how it ends, slams his forearms down on the keys, bends his head and succumbs to violent weeping. He doesn't know why.

When people meet Henry they excuse his chilly self-containment on the basis of his work, which is neither chilly nor self-contained. This is a true artist, they say, the reviews say: the true artist who pours his humanity into his art. But in Deep River, in Kramer, no one reads the New York Times. What of his chilly self-containment here? To whom can he say that the sight of almost any kind of body is enough to make you weep, sob, throw yourself to the ground, rend your clothing with joy, with sadness, with both at once. Watch anyone flex an arm muscle, wiggle a toe, sigh deeply, engage in love, sex, eating, sleeping, dancing – it is a palette he can work with, given music, his aider and abetter. In New York he is surrounded by fit bodies and young minds; beauty is never in doubt. Here, there are few fit bodies and young minds. What of beauty? Hector would say that it didn't exist here– he would look at the raped mountainsides and undernourished bodies, and make that judgment. But this is the place where as a boy Henry discovered beauty, in the landscape, and in his father's library, and in himself. In himself, he sees for the first time, because Bella – Bella, not Max - opened a dance school for hillbilly children. She is the true artist, not he. He has appropriated her soul.

They had given Bella a sedative and put her through all the uncomfortable tests. She hadn't felt a thing, but now that it is over and she is permitted to lie in a white bed unmolested by doctors and nurses, she finds herself adrift in an embryonic sac of feeling. Or is it memory? She can't tell.

"We're going to have a baby," she said to Max. They had been married for four years, long enough to believe it wouldn't happen. It was even more complicated than that, because Max had wanted a child at first but had come not to care, whereas she had been the opposite.

She had tried to find a nice time to tell him the news, but there were hardly any nice times by then. He didn't look at her anymore, and his infrequent use of endearments was either dutiful or ironic. She took care over dinner that night, but then he arrived home quite late and said he had already eaten in Kramer. He wanted to be left alone. So she put the uneaten meal away and washed the dishes. He was sitting in his chair in the living room, reading one of the old books that she had given him, that she had read but he hadn't. She had lost her taste for books, she told him. It was such a long time ago. She no longer felt educated.

She sat down on the edge of the sofa and said his

name, and when he ignored her she pretended she hadn't heard her and said it more loudly. He lowered the book and gave her that look, disdainful and familiar. It is an expression she sometimes sees in Henry's face.

"I'm tired, Bella. Can't you leave me in peace just one evening?" So then she had to blurt it out; there was no other way.

"We're going to have a baby."

Then he was kind. He put the book away, and smiled and dropped his voice to that low, soft, heart-catching tone he used to have, and came and sat beside her. But his attitude was fatherly and condescending, and she sensed his disappointment. She didn't understand, but accepted what he offered and demanded nothing more. She knew by now that what he gave he would eventually want back, with interest.

She had never demanded more, that was the trouble. She had thought she was when she married him – that she had been demanding a new and different life - and it had only proved how bad her judgment was. She had thought she was when she told him she would start the school, but he had belittled that too and then made it his, just like the books, and Henry. But she was the guilty party. She had let him do it. That was what the women in her family did, all of them, eventually. It was the curse she had thought to escape by coming to America with Max.The lucky ones married men who actually liked women so that it didn't matter so much. Later she couldn't even bear to remember the good times with Max, and there had been some, knowing what inevitably followed. Until the novelty had worn off, he had loved her. It would be easier never to have been loved at all. At least their child was a boy – he wouldn't be like her.

"It looks like you have acute leukemia, Bella," Dr. Roberts says. She is sitting up in bed with breakfast on the table across her lap, and Henry is sitting in the chair beside the bed. "There are a couple more tests we can run…" but Bella holds up her hand and shakes her head.

"You know better than to even suggest that, James. You've tested me enough, thank you, and we both know two more vials of my blood or urine fed to the mice – or whatever it is you do - won't make any difference beyond more money for the hospital. Now, I want to go home." She pushes the table away, and Henry stands up.

"Don't you want to know more?" Even Dr. Roberts is not quite prepared for her disinterest.

"No," she says firmly. "My grandmother had leukemia. I know what it's like and also that there's not much you can do that isn't unpleasant and ultimately futile. Better leukemia than some other things I can think of. And please don't go predicting my life expectancy– I'll figure it out as I go along, more fun that way. Now get out and let me dress. You too, Henry. I can manage on my own."

They waited in the hall outside her room.

"*Can* you say how long she has?"

Dr. Roberts's usually cheerful countenance is grave and sympathetic. "Not long I think, Henry. Up to six months, but probably less. With acute leukemia, the symptoms can come on suddenly and severely. It's probably why she fell yesterday. She's going to want to stay at home, you know."

"Then she will."

"You'll need to hire nurses; someone should be in the house with her all the time now, and it won't be long before she needs real nursing care."

Henry is surprised. "I'm in the house with her. I'll take care of her myself."

It is the doctor's turn to be surprised. "You're staying? What about your work?"

"I'm staying."

James Roberts contemplates the younger man for a moment. "I don't want to intrude, but I'm a lot older than you so I'm going to give you a piece of advice: don't isolate yourself in this, Henry – find yourself some friends."

Henry's answering smile is hollow. "Don't worry about me, Doc."

When they get home, he knows better than to be too solicitous. She is weak, though – weaker than she had been two days earlier. She wants to sit in the living room. He follows her in, still holding her little bag, and when she sees him standing there she laughs.

"Don't fuss, Henry, and don't hover. We'll get used to this. Just put my bag in the hall – I'll take it up later. Now go on – I know you have things to do."

He does as she says but takes her bag up to her room, then goes to his own. He had left the house early that morning to get to the hospital. He makes the bed now. He had wanted to tell Bella that he had cleaned the dance studio, that it shone now, that the record player still worked and everything else, but what is the point of telling her? He doesn't even know the point of having done it. He stands at the window and looks out at the lush new green, trying to imagine the days and weeks and months ahead. He can't. He will have to call Hector, who will be angry. He can't face it now; he'll do it tomorrow.

In the afternoon, Linda comes on her way home from her job at the bank in Kramer. Bella is sleeping on the sofa in the living room, so Henry leads her into the kitchen.

"I haven't been in this house in a long time," she says. "I always liked it. I'm sorry about Bella, Henry."

"About Bella? How did you find out so quickly?"

"He wanted me not to tell you – Doc Roberts stopped in the bank. He says you're staying. I came to say please don't lock yourself away up here – you'll go mad. You should hire some help."

"I don't need help." He sees her skepticism. "I'll hire someone later."

But she is firm. "You have to at least have someone on call, now. I know people; let me do it for you."

He knows she's right. "All right. Thank you, Linda."

She props her chin on the back of her hand and studies him while he begins preparations for his and Bella's supper. He is so self-contained that it is maddening; he allows no entrance at all. She remembers when Ruthie was small, he could make her laugh – he could make them all laugh with his understated and surprising humor. Surely he hadn't lost that ability. "Do you remember how you used to tease Ruthie into laughter?" she asks. "No one could do it like you."

She sees him smile. "Yes, I remember. We were all so contented then, in your little house. Ruthie was such a sweet baby, and Jack and I thought we ruled the world."

She takes a risk. "Don't be so afraid to open up a little, Henry."

He whips around, an appalling look on his face. "Don't say those kinds of things to me."

She has made him angry, but he stops what he's doing and sits back down at the table where he lays his head on his arms like a child. She waits and eventually he lifts his head and she sees his bleary eyes. She hasn't realized how exhausted he is. "Haven't you been sleeping?"

"Not much," he admits. "Linda, I don't want to talk about myself. You always used to be right about pretty much everything; you probably still are. But any discussion of me is irrelevant. Okay?" He smiles. "Let's talk about you."

She is hardly more comfortable than he is at self-revelation, and the conversation quickly dies under the weight of mutual restraint. Life has changed since fourteen years ago.

When she leaves, she says, "I'll find Bella a couple of nurses, and make sure they have good references. It won't be difficult – there are plenty of capable women dying for work around here. But promise you'll take care of yourself, Henry, and that you'll call me if you need anything." Wearily he agrees.

He brings his and Bella's supper into the living room on a tray, and neither of them eat. "You're tired," he says finally, and she admits it without any accompanying sarcasm. It is still light out, but she tells him good night and forbids him to go upstairs with her. "I won't fall, I promise." He hears her moving about and then the familiar creak of the board beside her bed announces that she's safely tucked herself in.

Henry takes the tray to the kitchen and cleans up, looks around the spotless room and has a moment of self-derisive angst. Just once, he wishes he would leave it all for the mice like Bella used to. He turns out the light and returns to the living room where he throws himself into the comfortable chair by the fireplace, that used to be Max's. Idly, he picks up the book lying on the table and opens it to the flyleaf: *Max Oliver.* He turns to the title page. It is Petrarch's Rime Sparse; seeing that he turns automatically to his favorite, number eighty and reads the last lines, which he doesn't have to read at all, since he knows them by heart: *Lord of my death and of my life/ before I shatter my ship on these rocks/ direct to a good port my weary sail.* It seems a hopeless proposition. Just as he lays the book down and is about to close his eyes, he hears footsteps on the porch and a knock on the door. Who, this time? At least in New York no one drops by uninvited. He wants to be left alone in his misery.

Nevertheless, he goes to the door and opens it.

It is the time of evening just before dark when everything is a monochrome wash, and he can't see distinctly, but even if he were able to the identity of the visitor would not have registered immediately.

Henry squints.

"Well, say something, damn it. Took me long enough to find this place."

It is Hector, who now steps in uninvited and envelops his star dancer in a bear hug that fills Henry with ambivalence. "What are you doing here?"

Hector ignores the question. He closes the door, and now Henry can see him. He is more rumpled than usual and, Henry is astounded to see, unnerved. But it brings about an improvement in his own manners, and he leads his unexpected guest into the living room. Hector looks around him. "So this is the old homestead. Nice, in a rural sort of way. I don't know what I expected. I don't want to impose, Henry, but do you have a bathroom, and then could I have something to drink – and possibly a bite to eat? I'll sleep here on the sofa, if that's all right. Don't worry – I'm on a flight back to New York tomorrow."

After Hector has eaten the dinner that Henry and Bella couldn't, he carries the dishes to the kitchen and leans against the doorsill while Henry washes them. "You eat better than I do," he says jocularly. "Who's your cook?"

"I am."

"And you've never had me over!"

It is too much for Henry. He hangs the dishcloth on its hook, takes Hector by the arm and leads him back to the living room. "I don't understand why you've come."

"To find out what the hell's going on, of course. And to see if I can't drag you back to New York for the opening. Of course I'm relieved that you'll be keeping off that knee, but you simply must take your bow for a masterpiece. Jesus, Henry. This is big – everyone's talking already."

Henry's smile is detached. "And what if everyone hates it?"

"They won't. You know perfectly well."

"Yes, I know. But it's only a dance."

Hector is silent. When he speaks, his tone balances between genuine concern and something like disgust. "This is because of Ray. You blame yourself – and me, for what happened, so now you're trying to punish us both. Henry, that is why I really came."

"Hector, do you remember when the Stonewall riots

happened, ten years ago? The Vietnam War? Were you aware of them at all while they were going on?"

" Well, the war – of course! Stonewall - sort of. I mean, it was hard to be totally unaware if you lived in the City. What's that got to do with anything?"

"Well, those events turned Ray into an activist. More than a substance abuser or a pretty good dancer, he was an activist – for world peace and human rights, not just gay rights. Lately I've been thinking about what he said to me once, because I was hardly ever aware of anything at all outside the studio and my own head, and he and I were close then. I didn't want to know – too distracting."

"What did he say?"

Henry laughs. "He asked me if I was just going to stay home all my life and listen to Purcell. And my reply was, what's wrong with that? We had an argument about art and politics. I said I kept them separate and he wanted to know how, because – one way or another – to him, art is politics, and vice versa. Even Purcell engaged in social commentary. I do, you do – we all do. He said I was the most out gay man he knew, because I just go along doing what I want, pretending nothing's wrong."

"So? What's wrong with that?" Hector wants to know.

"He thought it was a terrible waste." Henry leans

forward. "This isn't about Ray. I might have been able to do more to help him – I don't know. But I don't take full responsibility, and I don't blame you at all. What I'm trying to tell you is that it really *is* just a dance, and you all will get along fine without me there. I'm not coming for the opening Hector, and that's final. I suppose I'm sorry to miss it, but my regret is rational and unemotional – I don't think about it much at all. I probably won't be back for a few months. We found out this morning that my mother's dying. I'm all she has, and I don't want to stay in my room listening to Purcell anymore. I'm not leaving."

Hector nods his head slowly as his not-unsympathetic brain ingests Henry's words. "Well. Now I see – it's as though you knew, isn't it? That something was wrong. You would never have come back here otherwise. You've always seemed so glad to have escaped. I'm very sorry, Henry. How old is your mother?"

"She's sixty-three. Yes, I've always believed I had escaped. It all looks so different now, though. I'm learning by the minute."

Hector smiles, his brash façade muted by his understanding. "Seems to work that way, I'm afraid."

They sit in silence for several minutes, both of them too weary to make a further effort. When Henry hears the familiar creak of the floorboard above their heads, he speaks.

"You're tired – I am too. You don't have to sleep on the sofa – as it happens, there's an extra bedroom, and thanks to my being so anal it's nice and tidy. Come on, let's go up. You had better meet Bella."

She is just getting back into bed when Henry pokes his head in. "I know it's late, but I thought you'd enjoy a shock – we have a visitor. May I bring him in?"

Hector is not very many years younger than Bella, and he has long ago mastered the art of flirting. She is propped against the pillows when he enters and has, with Henry's help, made a cursory effort at sprucing up. Hector's quick eye takes in the room, the antiques – used rather than treasured – bathed in the soft light of the pretty old lamps, the clutter on the bedside tables, which even Henry has not attempted to discourage, the threadbare, once-fine old quilt, the woman herself. She does not, at first glance, in the least resemble her son, and yet there is something. He will have to think about what that something is. He strides to the bed, the floorboard groans, he takes her hands and kisses both her cheeks.

"I'm honored, Bella."

"Oh, bosh," she retorts. "This is a thrill for me, you know – rather dull in these parts, most of the time."

He sits in the Victorian rocker by the bed, and continues to hold her hand while Henry watches from where he has settled on the cedar chest at the foot of the old spool bed. There are a few moments of silence while Bella and Hector size each other up, and Henry is overcome with the oddly bittersweet sensation that it might be Max sitting there protectively holding Bella's hand in the golden light; that tragedy and time might not have separated them; that he, Henry, would still have them both; that it would have been different – Bella would have been different, a normal mother, less silly and eccentric, more motherly and gentle, as he imagined other mothers to be. He would have been different too – happy, able to care about the world outside himself. And Max. Max.

They are talking softly, he realizes.

"...I gave up the school not too long after Henry went up to Juilliard." She is answering a question of Hector's. "I guess he was my life's work – I never had another student come close."

"A great part of it is absorption, which some people call passion. If they don't have that, then the rest is irrelevant."

"It's a sad thing," Bella says. "But here, it seems to me, the children don't feel entitled to passion regarding anything of their own. They grow up in these mining towns and have their passion knocked out of them over and over. They come to fear for their own hopes and dreams early on. Henry was lucky."

"In that, yes. Even in a big city, the gifted students are few and far between. He was mostly lucky to have had you."

Bella looks down at their hands entwined on the coverlet. "Oh, I don't know. I always worried that what I could teach him was inadequate. I tried."

"Don't be so modest. He was what – sixteen? – when he left here? He was already formed by the time he came to New York."

"I often think, in his case, it was the stillness," Bella says.

"I beg your pardon?" She says something in German. Henry's surprise is such that he thinks he is dreaming, that he must have gotten trapped in some sort of dimensional irregularity. He knows what she has just said – it is in one of his father's books - but Hector doesn't.

"Talent builds itself in stillness; character in the storm of the world," she says. "It's Goethe. I used to love to read him, long ago. It's the character part that matters, really – more than the talent; I've been out of the storm of the world for so long that I must have negative character by now. But that's not the point. It was the stillness here that nurtured Henry's talent. I only hope the storm of the world has done as much for his character." She looks down the bed at her son. "Has it?"

Henry is brought back to reality by the familiar double-edged tone of the question. He stands up. "Not much," he says. "Your room is on the right as you go out of here, Hector. Good-night, you two. I'm going to bed."

Yet the thing that has struck Henry most is that Hector speaks to his mother as herself; that he sees her in some way that Henry never has and perhaps never will, and that he respects her. Henry has never respected her; he has never even thought about what it would have meant, to respect Bella.

He is drinking coffee in the kitchen when Hector appears and pours himself coffee before sitting down at the table. "How is Bella today?"

"Content," Henry replies, "but weak. She says you talked a long time."

"Was that bad?" Hector asks, worried that he might have undermined her already frail health.

"Not at all – she enjoyed it. Dare I ask what you talked about?"

"No – I'm not going to tell you. I'm glad I met her – makes this hair-brained trip worthwhile. She's lovely. You never told me she was English, Henry."

"Didn't I? I suppose I never think of her as English –

she never went back, you know, and none of her relatives ever seemed to take much interest in us. I think they're all dead now – not a long-lived family. I never met any of them."

"She's very well-educated. Impressive."

"What?" Henry asks in disbelief. "No, that's Max. She's just trying on some of his erudition for you." But her quoting of Goethe lingers in his own mind. She had not been parroting anyone, except perhaps Goethe.

"Well, anyway – I like her. You're very lucky to have such a mum, as I believe we established last night. But now I suppose I'd better call the cab company – my flight's at one, and they have to get all the way here and all the way back."

"A cab? What are you talking about?"

"How do you think I got here?"

Henry hasn't thought. "You took a cab? My god." He laughs until his eyes water.

Hector looks hurt. "What was I supposed to do?"

"I don't know – I must have thought you'd rented a car. I'll drive you to the airport."

Later, after Hector has said good-bye to Bella, he waits for Henry on the porch, where the view is almost the same as the one from Henry's bedroom window – a stunning panorama of the valley. "I can't believe you grew up here," he says to Henry when he joins him. "It's so incongruous – this impoverished, beautiful countryside set against your absolutely urban career. I don't quite understand how you came to be you."

Henry leans on the wrought iron railing. "I might have agreed with you a year ago, but I don't anymore," Henry tells him. "Ever since I left for New York, at the age of sixteen, people have asked me about growing up here as though it were a quaint hobby I'd chosen to pursue on a whim – "growing up in Appalachia." And then when I started to make my own dances, everyone was surprised that I'd ever even heard of Bach, Mozart, Webern, or Purcell, let alone that I would have the wherewithal to understand the music well enough to choreograph without making a complete fool of myself. But my earliest exposure to Bach, et al was *here*. And, yes, I had unusual parents, but if I had had the same parents somewhere else – New York, for instance – I would probably have turned out differently. The place matters too. And I used to be so ashamed of it."

Hector puts his hand on Henry's shoulder. "I'm not sure you're right, but I understand what you say. You've grown already, haven't you – being here these past few weeks? And you're warmer."

"Am I?" The expression on his face startles Hector, an odd mix of fear, yearning, self-doubt, and something else. Hope?

When Henry returns he finds Pete in the living room with Bella. He hears them chatting cheerfully when he enters the hall and is once again assailed by the depressing realization that everyone seems to enjoy his mother except himself. Hector's brief visit has stirred his need for a life beyond the narrow confines he has constructed. He would like to blame it on Deep River, but he knows he can't, so he is both happy and sorry to see Pete – happy, because he likes him and he is a diversion, and sorry because there is so little his presence can do to alleviate Henry's isolation. He rises when Henry enters.

"Bella says you've had a visitor."

Henry throws himself down into a chair. "Hector Gardner, our artistic director."

"Yes, your mother's been regaling me with tales."

"That sounds suspicious. What sort of tales?"

"All the things you never tell me," Bella says. "It was fun, for a change, sitting up all night talking. I like him, Henry."

"And he likes you. Did he tell you why he came?"

Bella hesitates. "I think because he was worried about you." Pete looks from one to the other of the two

112

guarded faces. "Well, I told him you're a big boy now and will do what you will do. Was I right?"

Henry is relieved and the tension dissipates. "Yes. Thanks, Bella. He can be very unpleasant at times, you know – however much he may have charmed you."

"Oh, I could tell that straight off," Bella replies, and winks at Pete, whom Henry addresses next.

"What are you up to?"

"School's out," he says, "so I'm footloose and fancy-free until summer school starts in three weeks." He gives Henry the slow grin that Henry is learning to recognize as mischievous. "Thought you might like to go hiking, fishing, something."

"Is it safe?" He has always had a horror of snakes.

"You've been in the city too long. It's safer than New York, I'd say."

"He's been telling me about Roy, Henry," Bella says in a strained voice.

"Roy?" The onslaught of memory feels like punishment – a fast rush of clear sight, he a six year old boy always watching, trying to help, while Roy builds that wall out back. And then he just disappeared from their lives with no explanation. One day there; the next day not, and that was that. "What of Roy?" he says to Pete, not

Bella.

And Pete tells him about Sarah, the daughter, and Roy's endless search for her. "This is the first time he's had word in a couple of years. I hope he finds her – at least, I guess I do. She's caused him a lot of worry over the years. Did you ever know Roy, Henry? He says he worked for your father."

Henry looks at his mother, and her eyes meet his and glance away. "When I was a boy, I knew him – but I haven't seen him since just after Max died. I suppose I never realized he had a daughter. I don't remember anything about her. So he's still around."

"He lives on my land, as a matter of fact. Built a little house on the far side, near the old school. He and I are good friends now. In fact, I should go. I'm looking out for his place while he's away, and I want to print some pictures before tonight."

"Taking Linda out?" Henry asks. Pete blushes.

"Yes, to the movies. We're going to see "Attack of the Killer Tomatoes." Want to come?"

Henry laughs. "I wouldn't dare."

Pete says goodbye to Bella and walks outside with Henry. "I'm sorry to hear the bad news about Bella," he says. "I don't need to say, do I, that I'm here to help?"

"Thanks, Pete."

"Henry, there's something I've been thinking about – besides fishing, I mean. Roy told me that after Max died, he tried to help Bella but she didn't want his help. She "took against him" were his words. If it concerns your father, I thought you might want to know that. The past is a mysterious place – every little tidbit counts when you're trying to work a puzzle. When Roy gets back – if he does – you might want to get to know him again."

4. PETE'S PROPOSAL

Driving home Pete thinks about Henry, as he often has since he returned. When he is with him he finds it hard to turn away. He loves to watch him move - his angular grace, the dark hair contrasting with the pale skin and eyes, the sensual but stubborn mouth; and to hear his low, clear voice, and what he has to say, and how he says it. He could ply him with questions for hours but fears to – fears intruding and being boring himself, fears coming to like him too much so that when he goes away again – which he is sure to do – he would miss him. Pete has many friends and acquaintances but has never had a close friend. He smiles as he sticks his hand out the window for a right turn. If Henry were a woman, why, he'd be half in love with him.

He parks on the grass under the elm trees as he always does and climbs the stone steps to where they meet the path to Roy's place, just beside the outhouse. From there he can see that someone is sitting on the workbench attached to Roy's cottage. It is Linda. Pete feels a twinge of regret, he doesn't know why – he is crazy about her, and they are going out later, but right now his mind is elsewhere. He sees her head turn and that she recognizes him, and he hurries forward. She stands up and crosses her arms as though it were a chilly day. When he reaches her and stands beside her before Roy's bench, she drops her arms to her sides; she is so homely that she's beautiful, he thinks, not knowing that his assessment of her is the same as Henry's. He puts his arms around her and kisses her.

"What are you doing here?" he asks.

"Stopped to see Roy on a whim," she replies. "I do, about once a year – at strawberry jam time."

They have never talked about Roy. "I can help you with the jam, but Roy isn't here. He went off to look for Sarah – you know about Sarah?"

Linda frowns. "I remember Sarah from when we were small – we were at the same church, before my parents decided that for middle class, light-skinned blacks like us, the church on the hill was too inconsequential. Sarah went away, didn't she?"

"Yes. She went away. Everyone says it was the hippies lured her off, years ago. Roy wants to find her of course, so he follows up on every lead."

Linda sits down on the workbench and runs her fingers along the rough surface of the grinding stone. "He's never talked to me about her."

She is disappointed, and Pete doesn't understand her disappointment. "He doesn't talk about her much.

Come up to the house," he says. "Let's have supper, then you can keep me company while I develop some pictures. By then, it should be dark enough for the drive-in, and I can protect you from the killer tomatoes."

Linda leans against the cool basement wall and watches Pete as he removes the dry prints from a line strung across one end of the basement room. "Do you think my family's weird?" she asks.

Pete is holding a print between the thumb and forefinger of each hand and studying it. "Sure. I think all families are weird, in different ways," he says. He knows she doesn't mean Ruthie. The words "family" and "weird" are practically synonyms, don't you think? I like this one." Carefully he turns the print around so she can see it.

It is a bird's eye view of Deep River. He shot it from the hill right above where the two rivers join. She knows the place – everyone does. It is where all the local teenagers go to learn drinking, smoking, and necking. The trampled down grass, the trees with their brashly inscribed trunks, and the mountain of accumulated litter cannot obscure the view, just as the poor houses and the narrow, pitted roads incised into the landscape cannot reduce its beauty. Pete's photographs always have a clear intent but not a simple one. He rarely photographs people, preferring to record their imprint upon the natural

118

world, or else the natural world alone. This one is typical: the evidence of human settlement -houses, roads, railroad tracks, the boom out to the dam – carefully antagonistic to the forested chaos and the fast-moving river and falls. The effect is beautiful and oddly disturbing.

Linda puts out her hand and traces the line of the road where it follows the river. Pete's eye follows her finger, notes it short, unpolished nail. "Do you like it?"

"Yes, I like it," she replies, "but why do you never shoot people?"

"I do weddings now and again," he objects.

"That's different – they pay you. It isn't art."

Pete laughs. "You call this art?" He lays the picture down on top of some others.

"Certainly I do," she says. "So do you, to yourself, when you don't have to pretend to be modest." Of course she is right. "You should get Henry to pose for you."

He turns back to the pictures remaining on the line, carefully removes a clip, and takes the next one down. "You think so?" he asks as he lays it down. She bends over to look at it.

"Why not? He'd be a good subject, in every possible way. It might be a diversion for him, too. People always build on rivers, don't they?"

"What?" Now Pete is thinking about Henry again.

"Rivers. What symbols they are to us all."

"Yes." He comes and stands beside her while she flips through the prints underneath those he has just finished, pulling out the ones she is interested in. She senses his protectiveness, not of her but of the pictures - they are his children and he doesn't quite trust her with them. In the middle of them all is one of Pete looking over the edge of a shabby roofline with a paintbrush in his hand. She laughs.

"This is nice, but you certainly didn't take it."

"No. I was up at the little church on volunteer day a couple of weeks ago – the Reverend snuck off with my camera and took it."

Underneath it are the ones he took behind the post office the day he ran into Henry. "Sperm?" Linda says in disbelief.

"Tadpoles, up behind the post office. Henry was with me that day." Does every topic lead to Henry? He draws her hand away from the pictures. "Come on, let's go upstairs."

"How much older are you than I am?" he asks suddenly while they are eating.

"I'm thirty-six," she says. "Seven years older than Jack – and Henry. You're a year younger than they are, right?"

He nods in affirmation.

"Why?" she asks.

"Do you think I'm too young?"

"Too young for what?"

"I don't know." She wonders what has gotten into him.

He refuses to let her help with their dishes, and so she follows him into the kitchen empty-handed. On the way past the corner cupboard she notices a framed photograph, picks it up and studies it. A pretty, determined teenaged girl.

"How is Mary Kay?" she asks. Pete comes and stands beside her. She feels the warmth of his breath around her head and since his earlier question is self-conscious of her dozen gray hairs.

"That picture's a few years old," he says, looking down at the photograph of his sister . "She's doing great – likes Pittsburgh. She's working hard, studying for the bar exam. There isn't much that would stop her." There is some sort of hesitation in his voice, but before Linda can speak, he continues. "I swore I'd do whatever it took –

beg, borrow or steal - to get Mary Kay a good education. She always was the smart one. "The smart one," that's how we defined her, as in "you're smart, you'll leave." Henry's like that. But you're smart and I'm not completely stupid - we're still here. But if I think about it much then being here starts to feel like I haven't made much of my life. Well, never mind."

"I know exactly what you mean," she says slowly. "I never thought in terms of making something of my life," she admits. "It's always been about someone else. Pleasing my parents, looking after Jack, and then Ruthie. But I'm a girl, and older than you – it goes with the territory. I was never very aware of other options." She isn't being entirely honest, but she doesn't correct herself. "Ruthie is the one of us who will leave, finally," she says. "I can't imagine her staying here. I don't want to think about it. Why didn't you visit Henry when you went to New York? He would have liked that."

He is surprised. "Why? We didn't know each other. I was a year behind – you know how that went, back then. And he and Jack were so unapproachable. I was just another gawky hick with my big feet and heart murmur and bad eyes – they were like a couple of young gods."

"Gods? Hardly the appellation I'd use. A couple of young fags seemed to be the more prevalent opinion."

"No one thought that besides Ricky Davies and a

few of his cronies."

"Plenty of people thought that," she says irritably. "They just didn't have the balls to say so – they let Ricky do it for them. Jack and Henry both got hate calls. After Henry left, Jack was cornered one night, and beaten to a pulp – you know about that. Henry still feels guilty about not being here, but why should he? It's a good thing he wasn't. They beat the shit out of Jack; they probably would have killed Henry. At the least it would have been very bad for his dancing. He wouldn't have known how to fight back the way Jack did."

"That may all be true," Pete concedes, "but plenty of others felt the way I did. Other kids trusted Henry and Jack, for all their difference. They had credibility. They had power, and not everybody resented it."

"If you and your friends felt that way, why didn't you prevent their being ostracized and mistreated?"

He has no acceptable answer. The demarcation line between the everyday and the unknown, between kindness and cruelty, is often so fine as to be imperceptible until one has already tripped over it. One can only hope to step more cautiously next time.

"I wish I'd known Jack," he says. "I wish I'd known both of them."

"I do too," she says, "but you still can get to know

Henry."

"I'm trying."

At eleven, when he drives her home from *Attack of the Killer Tomatoes*, and they once again discuss Henry, he decides to ask her to marry him.

"Why don't we just get married?" is how he puts it.

She promises to think about it.

A few days later, Pete goes to visit Bella and Henry. He parks in the Inn parking lot and walks from there; he hopes the exertion will clear his mind, which is confused from a chronic lack of sleep and continued astonishment at his own rashness. He has been up since five and awake since long before that, as he has done every one of the four mornings since he proposed to Linda. He should be walking on air, but this is quite a different sensation. At first he wondered if he had actually proposed or had only dreamed it. Now he wonders what he is to do about it. He takes refuge in the knowledge that she has not accepted but has only agreed to consider his offer, and yet he is twenty-eight, at an age to be married. They suit each other as well – are two of a kind. But they continue as though nothing has changed, without speaking of the other night or of the future.

The new situation, however understated, has afflicted him with a raging case of claustrophobia and he wants nothing more than to get away from people altogether. At dawn he had wandered up into the woods but it hadn't helped his restlessness, a state he is unable to identify satisfactorily. He returned to the house to make coffee and had then carried his mug down to Roy's. The chairs that Roy uses on the porch were locked inside the house, so Pete sat on the workbench with his back against the house and his knees drawn up, sipping his coffee. It was another nice day, promising to be hot though. Where is Roy now, he wondered. Perhaps he'd found his Sarah and was preparing to bring her home. If so, he would have to find some place for her to live – his own house is too small. With a shock Pete realized it could well mean that Roy would move – find a house somewhere big enough for both of them to live in and abandoned his little cottage here. He misses Roy and would miss him worse if that happened. Now he is on his way to see Bella and Henry. As people, they are the most removed of anyone he knows from the common stream of humanity, and he deludes himself into thinking that their otherworldliness might calm him.

Bella's Buick is parked in the old stone garage on the way up the hill, so he knows Henry hasn't driven off somewhere - he is the only one to use the car these days. Pete passes the garage and climbs the last steps to the walkway to the house. He stops for a minute to look at the view –no wonder Max Oliver insisted on building here.

The main door is sitting open. Pete peers through the screen and gives it a pull, but it is latched. He rattles it, and calls.

Bella comes slowly down the stairs into the hall and shuffles to the door. She peers back at him through the screen. Her face is taut with the exertion of coming downstairs, but the tension disappears the moment she sees who it is. She fumbles with the latch.

"Pete," she says. "I'm so happy to see you."

He steps inside the door and hugs her. It has been just a few days since he last saw her, but she is much thinner; he feels the delicate bones of her back through the thin gown. "Did I get you out of bed? I thought Henry was here." He holds on to her, worried that his grip will hurt her but afraid to let go. "I can help you back upstairs."

She is as sharp-tongued as ever though. "Christ, Pete, don't fuss. I'm sick of the bedroom anyway. Same four walls the whole damn day. Let's go in the living room, then you can put your arm around me and hold my hand." She coyly catches his eye and winks, which only makes him more sharply aware of the illness and probable pain she is attempting to hide.

"Nothing I'd like better."

It takes them ages to get to the living room. He settles her on the sofa and hovers above her. "Let me get you something to drink," he says.

"Stop it, Pete. Sit down." She pats the cushion beside her.

He does as he is told, and she nestles her head into his shoulder. He puts his arm around her, takes her hand. It's what she wants.

"I don't know where Henry is," she says. "He has a place up on the hill, where he's gone since childhood. He may be there. He won't be long – he thinks I can't do without a babysitter." The idea obviously disgusts her, but Pete is relieved to hear it.

"You can tell he's moved back, can't you? A place for everything and everything in it's place with him around. He's always been like that, in complete rebellion against my slovenliness."

Pete laughs. "It's not rebellion, it's just his nature. He was born neat. Some people are."

"You think so? How comforting. Were you born neat?"

"Middling," says Pete.

"Well – strictly between you, me and the bedpost - I kind of like him keeping house. His orderliness is soothing, but I pretend not to notice that he's spent hours scouring the kitchen and bathroom."

"Why do you do that?"

"I've always chided him about his neatness; it wouldn't do to stop now."

"You don't think it hurts his feelings?" She hasn't considered her behavior from that perspective. "You think I should thank him?"

"Sure. Why not?"

"Because it might reinforce his determination to stay and see me out."

Pete is caught off guard and Bella laughs at him. "Oh come on Pete, don't look so appalled. It's all right – I don't mind going, but I do mind my son jeopardizing his career. He doesn't belong here. He belongs back up in New York." For effect, she pauses, so that her best pronouncement is deliberately startling. "His latest thing is that he's going to re-open my old school. Can you imagine such absurdity?" Pete is silent. He is thinking of the conversation he had with Linda one night, about the smart people always leaving. "Well?"

"I think it's his call," Pete says stubbornly. "What's so wrong with staying here? We all did."

"What is this, a conspiracy? It's my fault he's here

– you should have heard me on the phone to him month after month with my wheedling and whining. It wore him down. I wanted him to come for all the wrong reasons – to prove I still had some say in my own family, I guess. But now that he's here I want him to go, and that's for the right reason: so he doesn't mess up his own life."

"You know, Bella – I don't actually believe you." He decides to be, according to his lights, ruthless. "From what you've told me, I'd say you saw this as your last chance with Henry – and as his last chance with you."

Bella is silent.

"Henry's got things going on in his head too, Bella; he's got his own problems, his own questions. Maybe he needs to be here with you right now for himself, not only for you. You just let him do what he needs to do, okay?" He knows he is right about this.

She seems to believe him, but then she asks him a peculiar question. "And should I tell him what he needs to hear, do you think? Even if it hurts him and turns me once and for all into a liar?"

They hear the faintly irregular footsteps and then water running in the kitchen. A moment later Henry is standing on the landing above them, wiping his wet face with a clean dish towel, and Pete feels as a reflection of his own expectation the change in Bella's body at the sight of her son.

"Hello, Pete."

Henry comes down the shallow stairs into the living room. His limp seems to have improved, or else he is controlling it. He settles into the chair opposite, his father's chair, and crosses his be-sneakered feet on the shabby ottoman.

"Where've you been?" Bella asks him. She is pouting.

"Just up on the hillside," he says. There is dust on his shoes.

"It's dry for so early in the summer," Pete comments. "I hope it's not a year for forest fires."

"When you were a little boy," Bella says to Henry, " you were so scared of the snakes, but you'd still go up there to that place of yours."

"I'm still scared of snakes, " he replies, "at least the poisonous ones. Have you been here long, Pete?"

"Not long. I didn't want Bella to think I'd forgotten her," he fibs.

"You're better than a son," Bella says, patting Pete's knee. He is embarrassed and tries to rise.

"I should go," Pete says, flustered. He hasn't seen Bella like this – angry, he thinks, and a little vicious, but Henry doesn't seem to pay attention. Pete had thought they would be calming, but together they are nerve-wracking.

"Have a glass of sherry with me," Bella protests. "Henry, bring the sherry."

Grinning, Henry rises and crosses to the table where the decanter sits, pours a glass of its amber contents and holds it up. "Pete?"

He shakes his head. "None for me. I really do have to be going." This time he manages to rise, leaning over to kiss Bella. Henry brings the glass and sets it on the table beside his mother, but she ignores it.

"I'll walk out with you," Henry says. As they let themselves out onto the porch, Bella's scraping voice follows them. "Don't be long, Henry."

When they are outside, Henry stops Pete. "Don't go yet. Walk up the hill with me – it might do us both good. I'm sorry about that little scene – it's her fear, you know. She acts it out instead of admitting to it. And she won't drink the sherry – that's for effect. She's stopped drinking and smoking both, although she still pretends, even for me."

"You take it pretty well."

"Bella and I have never spoken honestly with each other – it's always been these kinds of stupid games, and I've always hated it, but now I see her forgetting to

131

uphold her end of it half the time and I'm stricken with panic. We actually talk sometimes lately – it's very difficult, though, to break old habits. That little outburst inside was for your benefit." Henry smiled and looked down at his hands. "I think she wants you to know how much you mean to her."

"I watched my dad get sick and die," Pete says. "He wouldn't ask for help – we had to second guess him and then force him to accept it. You'll let me know if there's anything I can do?"

Henry nods distractedly. "Thanks," he says. "She wants to die at home – I've promised her she will."

"She says you're talking about reopening the school."

"I thought it might be an interesting experiment," Henry says. He is ahead of Pete on the path, so Pete can't see his face or tell how serious he is.

"But you won't be here that long."

"Who knows?" Henry replies. "I can stay here forever if I choose to, and what is necessarily so terrible about that?" It is so close to Pete's own earlier thoughts that he gasps. "I have no sense at all right now of that other life of mine. Do you know they are premiering my new piece tonight? It's the talk of the town, apparently – and has been sold out for weeks. I don't feel anything, nothing at all. That's someone else's life. Mine is here, now. With Bella."

"Only that isn't someone else's life," Pete demurs softly. "It's yours, too. You may not need to face it now, but you will eventually, whatever you decide you're going to do."

He doesn't know if he's annoyed Henry or not. They continue to walk in silence and after a few more minutes, Henry stops, studies Pete with his disconcerting gaze and at last responds to what Pete has said. "I know."

"Now come on," he adds and begins to climb again. His knee is remarkably well. "Here we are." Moments later he reaches up to grasp the thick curtain of wild grapevine before them. He pulls it away and steps aside to let Pete go first.

"Welcome to my domain," he says lightly, following Pete through and allowing the curtain to ease back into place.

They are in a small, perfectly rectangular clearing that has been delineated by neat stone walls on its uphill and downhill sides, by a stone slab and by the grapevines. Its floor is mossy and bright green, in contrast to the rough surrounding undergrowth. Completely hidden and shadowed, the clearing welcomes the thin rays of filtered and dancing light the way a disused old-fashioned parlor might welcome the sudden appearance of a young girl in her fine lace dress, as something beautiful but superfluous.

"Why is the ground so mossy here?" Pete asks.

"Why do you think?" Henry says lightly. "This place is enchanted." He goes to sit on the stone slab and looks up at Pete.

"Is that your sacrificial altar?"

Henry rubs the smooth stone. "Perhaps. Come sit on it and find out." He bends down to untie his shoes as Pete comes and sits on the roomy surface. "Take your shoes off. There's no sense in being in a place like this if you can't feel it under your feet." Pete does as he's instructed and finds the moss to be soothing on his calloused soles. He listens to Henry's soft voice telling him things that seem like secrets. Secrets.

"I've been coming here ever since – ever since my father died. This slab was here, believe it or not. I built the walls myself, after having carefully observed Roy Bright's work down around the house. It took the whole summer to bring the rocks here - there are plenty of them in the woods. This place saved me. I do think it's enchanted; I've never felt alone here, which may be why I've never felt the need to share it with anyone. You're the first person I've ever brought here."

"Not Jack?"

"Jack and I had another place we went together." His voice turns chilly. "On the Island – you know where I mean.

"I brought my father's books up here and read them. You can stretch out on this moss and it's as good as a bed – softer even. I never worried here, and I still don't. Like Hippoclides, in the Herodotus tale." He moves from the stone to the ground and stretches out on the moss on his back, stares up into the trees with his hands folded on his flat stomach, and continues to speak.

"In the eighteenth century, grottoes were the fashion of the wealthy. They would have these little exotic caves built, good only for firing or soothing the over-bred imagination. I've seen a few of them, when I've had time off while on tour – most of them are too cluttered, too decorative for me. But there's something about the idea – this is my grotto, only nicer – it's for the under-bred rather than the over-bred imagination, with the added bonus of a perfect window on the world. Go look." He raises an arm and motions toward the downhill side. "You may have to push some vines aside."

But Pete doesn't have to – he can see clearly through the branches. They are very far up the mountain now, and the panorama is more splendid, more mysterious, and absolutely silent. Nothing better obliterates the quotidian as utter silence, but in the end noise returns, always from the towns, the human habitats.

He doesn't say so to Henry. His grotto for the under-bred *is* a magical place, capable of neutralizing judgment and necessity for a time – but only for a time. It can never be permanent; it shouldn't be. He turns around to say something to Henry.

Henry is watching him from his place on the ground, but he has turned on his side, and is leaning on his elbow. "Sometimes I think this little place is the entire reason I keep coming back. My past, my present and my future. Will you let me know if Roy comes back? I'd like to talk to him. He was here, after Max died. Bella doesn't talk about it, but I remember him being here."

"I'll let you know when he comes back," Pete says as he turns his back on the view and comes to sit on the ground near Henry's head. Henry rolls onto his stomach and crosses his hands under his head. "I could easily fall asleep," he says and closes his eyes.

The minutes pass, and Pete sits cross-legged beside the still figure. He can't keep a thought in his head - that is part of the enchantment of the place. He supposes that it's different for Henry, who used to bring books here to read, but perhaps it is different for everyone at different times – perhaps it is a place that fulfills whatever current need one brings to it, so that one can return refreshed to the world of no enchantment. Almost without realizing what he is doing, Pete takes his glasses off and lays them on the slab. He brings his hand to Henry's head and strokes the straight dark hair and then, with the tips of his fingers, the fine neck. He runs the tip of his index finger along the cheekbone and traces the line of his jaw, runs his whole hand through Henry's hair, pushing it away from his face. Henry's eyes are open now; they look darker than they normally do, but they are welcoming, happy even. He turns on his side again so that he can reach out his arms and pull Pete down beside him, and their arms can go around each other comfortably. They remain like that, wholly still within the utter silence, for what might have been either a very long or a very short time – it doesn't matter which. Whenever it is that they stir, a long or a short while later, they do not speak until after they have returned their feet to their shoes and lifted the curtain of vines to face the harsher light outside. Pete says, "I want to photograph you. Linda says I never photograph people – she sees it as a fault that I should remedy." He senses that he has annoyed Henry; he has been the one to break the spell. Well, it was inevitable. He is not an otherworldly person the way Henry is. "May I?"

Henry has gone ahead of him again. He doesn't look back, but he says, "yes."

The events of June coincided with the direction of the weather, creating a precedent. The atmosphere warmed uncomfortably and in conflict with the cooler earth, setting up inversions to befuddle bodies and minds. These were rarely broken by thunderstorms, although thunder could frequently be heard in the distance, giving unfulfilled promises of violent release. It would seem to come closer then cease suddenly, having never disturbed the sultry blue of the sky. The remainder of the summer was hot and parched. The falls at Deep River dried up, the current of the river slowed, and the water that used to lap cleanly at the banks assumed the appearance of sludge and began to smell like rotting fish. Everyone went around with as many buttons as possible unfastened, wiping away the perspiration with one hand and fanning themselves madly with a folded piece of paper in the other. After July 4th, no one went swimming in the river though. Someone came down with typhoid. It wasn't a region where people had air conditioning – with so little money, and so many trees, caves, and rock cliffs there had never been any incentive for it.

Only Henry thinks in terms of musical rather than atmospheric inversions, of contrapuntal melodies, of intervals. In any given summer New York is hotter than this, and he is used to perspiring when he works. He is also used to the sense of separateness, and of exercising a will power that none of his Deep River acquaintances can come close to imagining. He has hired two women whom Linda recommended and gradually increased the time they spend at the house; Bella, whose condition seems to fluctuate without any definitive downturn, is surprisingly meek about it. Hiring the women has freed Henry to drive into Kramer and spend time in the studio, working out and toying with the idea of reopening the school. One day he drives into Charleston, forty miles away, where he purchases a new record player to replace the one he had broken, and a stack of records, not his usual fare: Doc Watson, Hazel Dickens, Ralph Stanley, Norman and Nancy Blake, and Hank Williams. He brings them back to the studio and listens carefully while he waits for Pete to arrive. They meet at the studio nearly every day during these two sweltering months, during which there are no "events," merely a holding pattern.

When they are together Pete and Henry talk about nothing that has to do with Deep River or its other inhabitants. They talk only about themselves, about dance, music, photography and books, and in detail about all of them. Pete learns more about dance and music in these two months than he ever dreamed of learning in a lifetime, and Henry's lessons in photography are of like intensity. They are equals when it comes to books, and they throw synopses and analyses of favorite work at each other like spitballs. The studio is its own inversion, a world apart, a world in a cloudbank, a world in a dream. There is no conflict here; it is perfect. Linda and Bella and even Roy might as well not exist.

Henry of course is an expert at going in rooms and shutting doors. Pete is not.

5. RECOVERIES

"Mr. Bright." The receptionist stands in the doorway of her cubicle and casts an eye around the crowded waiting room. When Roy rises hesitantly to his feet she beckons him toward the door leading to the doctor's office. He never gets used to coming here, no matter how many times he does it.

Dr. Cohen is beginning a mustache to go with his Beatles haircut. Roy wants to ask him why he is growing it; it makes him look even more like a teenager and he should realize that it is having the opposite effect from the one he intends.

Dr. Cohen stands politely and invites Roy to sit in the chair opposite him. He is smiling, as he does when he is not overly worried about conveying bad news. Roy has thought he is one of those white men – there are increasing numbers of them – who believe they must compensate for slavery. But Dr. Cohen is Jewish, he has that look, exotic and hunted; Roy can't imagine he has anything to compensate for. His family were probably in Hungary or Russia being persecuted too at some point in the last ninety years.

"Sarah is coming along well," he is saying to Roy, who has learned in the past six weeks that it's easier to understand what they're trying to tell you once you've skipped over large portions of the actual words. "She can be discharged on Friday." He almost misses that part, he is so used to vagaries. "The judge says you've agreed to be responsible. The charges have been dropped." Dr. Cohen frowns down at the paper on his desk then looks at Roy. "I thought you were her father. It says here you're not."

"No, Sir, I'm not her father. I raised her though, since she was a baby. She thinks I'm her father." But he doesn't want to explain. "I can take her home then."

"Home?" Dr. Cohen has forgotten.

"We're not from here, remember?"

"That's right. Yes, you can take her home, but you should enroll her in a program there. The recidivism rate is high, for heroin. What's the town again?"

"The town where the hospital is located is called Kramer. Charleston is forty miles away."

"Do you have a car?"

"No, Sir. But there's a bus."

Dr. Cohen looks tired. "All right. I'll see what I can find out about programs in that area and let you know on Friday."

Roy leaves the hospital and walks the three miles to where he has rented himself a room. Dear God, what's he going to do, in this one room here, with Sarah and

141

barely enough money to feed himself? At first, he had been doing a little yard work for people, but with the heat there is no pretending he is any younger than his seventy-one years. It was dangerous for him to work, the woman who had hired him said when she let him go, and she was right.

Back in his room, he counts what he has. There is enough for one and a half train tickets, and maybe a couple of apples. He looks around the room and wonders what he can do to make it decent for the two of them, just for a while. Long enough to earn a little more money. Then he goes out to scour around for a job. He finds one as a night watchman up at the college, and if he's budgeted half-way decently, there will be enough so that they can leave by the end of September if he can't think of another solution. That's only four weeks.

On Friday he goes to get her. She has been discharged already and is waiting for him in the lobby. He sees her through the window, her shoulders slumped in defeat. She is a tiny little thing, still almost beautiful, even after everything she's done to herself. A wave of mixed emotions washes over Roy, and he can't tell his love from his pity, or his pity from the revulsion he feels.

He has done what he can about the room: pushed the single beds apart and hung a curtain down the middle, repaired the lone chair that sits by the window. Out the window is a tree, and that is nice, and at least the room is spotless. She hardly notices though, and he is thankful. She sits down on the chair by the open window and puts her long-fingered little hands on the sill. They hardly know each other now, but he can tell she hasn't changed – that this illness, the drugs and the withdrawal, have just masked her natural solitariness and the way her mind goes wandering. Maybe when they get home he should mention that to her new doctor. When they get home, he'll have to do something about his house there too, or else find another one. Always something to do something about.

It's what Bella calls a 'weak day,' but she has come downstairs on her own while Mary, the nurse who is on duty, is washing the lunch dishes. She peeks into the kitchen. "I'll be in the living room, Mary," she says, and ducks out again quickly before Mary can natter at her. Bella is enjoying getting to know these nurses, although they aren't nurses – just country women wanting to earn some money. It's a new experience, having women in the house. The other one's name is Pat, and Bella likes her better – she never natters.

Bella has a hankering to reread all her old books, but where to start? She walks to the bookshelf and looks, runs her hand along the spines. Many of them are old and had once belonged to other members of her family. It was nice of Adrian to send them, but his taste in literature was far less eclectic than hers and none of these would have interested him. Taste in literature. She doesn't think she has any tastes at all anymore. Life in these parts, between rock cliff and river, the poverty and narrowness of experience, has stripped her of taste although it has done wonders for her compassion. She doesn't choose a book, not feeling quite up to seeing Max's name on the flyleaf of any she might pick. Instead, she sits down in Max's chair, which is closest to the shelves, and thinks about books. That's better. She sees her own hand, much younger, opening one of the volumes of Ovid to a tale of change which even then she had already read a dozen times. She used to cover the English translation with a piece of paper, determined to think of the story in Latin. Now, nearly forty years later, she finds she can still see the words: *Pyramus et Thisbe, iuvenum pulcherrimus alter, altera, quas Oriens habuit...* The truth is that Bella had been a hopeless romantic in her youth and as time proved the futility of such a view she learned to cover it up with silliness and sarcasm. But one view was as unpleasant as the other. It is, she feels, the *language* of romance that is so seductive, and when one is young one refuses to see the sharp edges, the precipices. Even when one falls off, one doesn't see them because it is already too late.

It doesn't matter anymore, though, and she finds much comfort in this discovery, that she can sit in Max's comfortable chair and shut her eyes and imagine the contents of every book she ever cared about.

An hour later, Mary comes in and brings her a cup of tea. "Would it be all right if I go, Mrs. Oliver? It's five now, and your son will be back by six."

Bella waves her hand, disoriented by the interruption. "Of course it's all right. I'm fine on my own."

But Henry isn't back by six and Bella, weaker than she will admit, struggles up the stairs to her room. She rests on the edge of her bed but needs to get to the bathroom so edges her way from bed to chair to wall all the while knowing that her bladder is going to outwit her dignity. It happens just at the threshold of the bathroom and makes her so angry that she ignores her weakness and starts across the large old-fashioned room to run a bath in the claw-footed tub. Even as she is falling her defiance doesn't fail her, and she loses consciousness with a strange sense of triumph.

Henry comes home at eight and is puzzled that there are no lights in the windows. He calls out as he comes in through the unlocked back door and switches on the light. "Mary? Bella?" Sure when there is no response that Mary has had to rush his mother to the hospital, he none the less makes a running search through the house.

"I'm here," calls a quavering but determined voice from the bathroom. He switches on the light to find his mother on the floor leaning against the bathtub and blinking up at him.

"Felled by my own piss," she says.

"Oh Jesus, Bella." He stoops beside her, one hand on the back of her head, one at her waist and pulls her gently to him – she has all the weight and spring of a rag doll, but the expression on her face, which he does not see, is potency itself. All the humiliation is worth it for this, her son's total submission to the instinctive rules of love.

"I'm not hurt," she assures him quickly, "but I'm wet. I didn't knock myself out – I fainted I'm afraid. A bad day. I wanted to take a bath."

"You still can," he says as he leans over to drop the plug into the drain and run the water. She is sitting in her own urine and needs to be cleaned up anyway. She has on only a loose-fitting dress over her underclothes, and he eases it out from under her and begins to pull it upward so that he can remove it over her head. He feels her hesitation and stops. He speaks gently. "Do you remember all the times in my life when you've come into my bedroom and glared at my poor unprotected nakedness and claimed your right, as my mother, to do so – the last time being about two months ago? You can think of this in the same way." She tries to roll her eyes, and lets him continue. He lifts her under the arms and legs and sets her in the shallow water, where he helps her to wash. For perhaps the first time in his life he understands that he sprang from this small, wasted body – a body that once, like his own, could execute all sorts of astonishing leaps and turns; a body connected to a mind that, like his, must once have dreamed of flying, since dreams are what drive one to such punishing lengths.

He lets the water run out and lifts her with two towels wrapped around her. She is shivering in spite of the heat. He takes her into the bedroom and puts her in the bed, where he helps her into a clean nightgown. When she is tucked under the covers, he sits down on the edge of the bed and gently combs out her tangled, faded hair – curly and red, so different from his own. When he is done, she looks at him gratefully and closes her eyes. Henry lays the comb on the table but remains where he is, his mind trembling under the pressure of all that is bearing down on it. The floodgate is about to open, the cap of the atmospheric inversion about to break. But all he hears is music, brilliant, threatening. This is a textural inversion.

Only later does he wonder why Mary isn't there.

He spends most of the night in the chair by Bella's bed. He knows without anything being said that the downturn has happened; that Bella has begun her slide toward the end. He knows because he suddenly feels very small and afraid, like a child left alone at the school door on the first day. Toward dawn, he stirs and gets up to check on her. Her eyes are open. He sits down beside her, and she lays her hand in his lap where he can take it without even thinking. Everything has changed between them, and it is the moment before dawn, when inhibition is at its lowest ebb.

"Why haven't you ever talked about your family, Bella?" It isn't a reproach, just a question. "You must have missed them. You never saw them again." Yesterday, if Henry had been told he would never see Bella again, he would have shrugged philosophically. Today is different.

She hasn't slept deeply. All night long she has been in that state halfway between waking and sleeping, the state that, when all is said and done, is most real. She would like to remain there, wedged between the various promises of life instead of having to live with the actual results of their non-fulfillment. She looks at the pale profile of her son, his head bent over. But he is a promise fulfilled, isn't he? The others don't matter.

"I wonder if I'll have time now to tell you everything,' she says. "Oh, not that so much happened. Nothing much did, really – we weren't one of those soap opera families." She smiles, and he smiles back. "My family was not very big, but it was very rich until the war. Upper middle class, I suppose you'd say. Respectable and conventional. I wasn't close to my parents – they were one of those couples who were so involved in each other that they shouldn't have had children. A bad example for Adrian and me. My brother Adrian was nice, but we weren't close either. I was the black sheep, you see. Not only did I dance in a professional theatre, but I did things like support striking workers. I never told you that before.

Yes, Henry, I was an activist. Go ahead, laugh. Part of my activism was marrying your father – moving to America seemed very daring to me back then. I didn't know."

"Didn't know what?" Henry asks. He sees that she is drifting.

"That marriage and daring have nothing to do with each other. Marriage tamed me, Henry. It might not have, if I had stayed where I had roots, but I don't know. My brother Adrian made a bad marriage too – he was several years older than I but died of a heart attack in his forties. Heart problems ran in the family. I'm sure he was homosexual, and hid it. At least you don't do that."

"Do you mind, Bella?" They have never discussed his orientation.

Bella laughs. "Mind? It's more complicated than that, isn't it? If I thought you wanted a domestic life and couldn't have it I would mind– but I know a little about what it means to have work that you love. It compensates – and complicates. I have to admit though – all that business with Jack Paisley in high school would have been enough to give a normal parent a heart attack."

"You said your brother made a bad marriage *too*. I thought your marriage with Max was a good marriage – wasn't it?"

She shouldn't have said it. It was a careless slip.

"Oh, well, all marriages have their problems, Henry." It seems like a betrayal of the spirit of dawn, but they both let it go.

"I've never seen you dance, Henry – not since you were a boy. I wish I'd taken you up on one of those invitations to New York."

"Why didn't you?"

"Because I've been here too long – New York seems far away."

Henry doesn't hide his disgust. "You mean you were afraid of coming to New York, just like all the other hicks. Bella! You aren't like that."

"It's too late now," she reminds him. "Let's talk about something else."

She dozes off, and Henry goes downstairs to make coffee and call the doctor. "Well," says Doc Roberts, "we both knew it was inevitable." Henry carries his coffee outside and sits on the wall. The sun is just rising above the hills, promising another hot day in spite of it being the first of September. There isn't much time, he thinks, for all the questions erupting in his brain. He had better put them in order and ask them.

"Why weren't you here when I got home last night?"

he asks Mary when she comes. He stops short of firing her. "But I will fire you if it ever happens again. If I'm late, you stay – that was our agreement."

On the way to the studio he stops in at the bank where Linda works. She is surprised. "Can we talk?" he asks.

"Not here – we'll be interrupted. But it's almost lunch time – let me tell my boss I'm stepping out."

They cross the street to the old drug store cum soda fountain and Linda orders a sandwich. "You aren't eating? You've lost weight since you've been here, Henry, and you can't afford to lose much more."

"Even Bella doesn't say such things to me, Linda. I could order something just to make you happy, but you would have to eat it. I'll have a Coke."

"I haven't seen much of you in the last two months," she says, "and I know you aren't spending all that time with Bella because I talk to Mary and Pat. What have you been doing?"

"This and that. Errands. I spend part of everyday at Bella's old studio – just trying to keep a hand in. Sometimes I imagine opening that old place; it would be so strange, wouldn't it, to be doing what Bella did. Maybe some little boy would come along that I could make a star out of." He blushes, and Linda laughs.

"Or girl," she suggested. "I don't see very much of Pete lately, either." She knows she sounds a little too casual.

"No?"

"Do you?"

"He stops by sometimes," Henry replies. To himself he sounds blatantly evasive.

"I suggested he photograph you -thought it might break him of his inanimate phase. Did he ask you about doing it?"

"He's taken a few photographs," Henry says, also too casually.

"Well, for someone who wanted to get married two months ago, he makes himself pretty scarce. Maybe he's changed his mind." Her effort at nonchalance fails, and Henry, who has been warily skirting her questions, looks shocked. "What's wrong, Henry? Is it so shocking to think someone might want to marry me?"

He recovers quickly. "Not at all. I just – didn't know. Did you say yes?"

"No. I haven't given him an answer. It isn't mad passion between us, but we would be a comfortable pair, I think. He's the nicest man I've ever known, and the best. Oh well, it's not your worry – I'll have to tackle Pete myself. What did you come to see me for?"

"Bella's worse. She's much weaker, just in the past day or two, and she fell again last night. No one was there. I was late getting home, and Mary had left. That won't happen again. I almost believe it's good that it did happen – I sat up with her last night, and it gave me a chance to think. I've become more forgiving of Bella – it's strange, but last night when I was putting her to bed she didn't seem like the same person I've rejected all these years. I've never known her. She told me this morning that she used to march in workers' strikes when she was young – can you imagine? I would never have dreamed it. But I've never dreamed anything about her at all – to me, she's always been a slightly dumpy little woman, my mother, who once ran a third rate ballet school."

"Third rate? I'm a little surprised to hear you say that, considering where you've got to. Statistically, a school like your mother's should never have produced one single student like you. You say you've become more forgiving, but of what? What does she need to be forgiven for?"

"I know, I know. You've said this kind of thing before." Henry's mouth has hardened in a way Linda remembers from long ago. 'She doesn't need to be forgiven for anything, but..."

"But whether you mean to or not you still blame her for Max's death. You think he was the origin of everything

153

good in your life, don't you? Maybe he was, I don't know, but he's been dead for twenty-five years, Henry. You don't even really remember him – you only imagine that you do, because you happen to have a mother who embarrasses you. Give yourself and Bella a break."

Henry pulls out his billfold and puts a five dollar bill on the counter. "Lunch is on me," he says as he stands up. "I didn't want to get into all that old stuff. You sound a little bit angry yourself. I wanted to tell you that I spent half of last night thinking about how good you were to Jack and me – neither of us could have gotten along without you. I haven't been a very good friend, and I'd like to try to do better, but this doesn't seem like much of a start."

"Sit down, Henry." He glares at her. "I'm sorry. You're right, I am being hard on you – a little. I'm just feeling cranky lately – it's this weather, and work, and fretting over Ruthie, and wondering why Pete's suddenly cooled off. Not to mention the distance you've been keeping and a sort of chronic loneliness."

Henry sits back down on the stool. "It's probably all the weather's fault," he says to lighten the atmosphere. "It's bound to break soon, don't you think? It's September."

They talk about unimportant things, but it is a careful peace they have made with each other. They say good-bye in front of the bank. "I know a woman who prefers doing night shifts," Linda tells him. "She's decent enough, and if Bella is worse, you should have someone there a few nights a week, so you can get some sleep."

He nods. "Yes, please. If she's available, that would be great."

He nods to the taciturn man at the service station and lets himself into the studio. He crosses the room to the record player and puts on some Bach then goes to stand in front of the mirror where even he can see that he's lost weight. As he works his way through a long series of warm-up pliés, relevés and battements, he studies his reflection for more than good form. The insulated world that he, or he and Pete together, have made here is coming to an end. All the decisions to be made and responsibilities to be upheld are about to become urgent if they haven't already. Emotion is going to seep in, only not *his* emotion. He doesn't feel a thing he tells himself furiously, and hasn't, except for that brief flicker of recognition when he was bathing Bella. He thinks of Linda's words, that Pete is the nicest and best man she's ever known. Would she still think that if she knew the truth? He can read the depth of Pete's emotion – it is right on the surface of his skin – but he knows perfectly well that Pete can read nothing of Henry's own, and that because there is none – no depth, no emotion. Is it all the busy years in New York, dancing, working long exhausting days, that have stripped him so? He should go back there, where many people are the way he is and it doesn't matter so much – hurting people is all part of the game. And yet he thinks about staying here, reopening the school – it is a sort of lethargy. He is struck suddenly by a memory of the old repetitive nightmare; now apparently he is living it, and is it really so bad? There's great peace in not striving. Well, he must make some sort of effort, keep up appearances.

He does a final plié, changes the record, and begins to leap and spin senselessly up and down the room. When Pete comes, he has to bring up with him his offer to Linda of marriage. That alone will demolish their little cocoon.

Only Pete doesn't show up that afternoon.

When Henry is beginning to wonder why he hasn't come, there is a tentative knock on the door. He opens it to a bedraggled, ill-dressed woman holding an eight year old child by each hand. They are too old to have their hands held, but she doesn't seem to know what else to do, and neither do they. She is nervous. The children look up at Henry curiously, and he smiles at them.

"May I help you?"

"Is this the ballet school?" she asks and then blushes seeing the puzzlement in Henry's face. She starts to leave, yanking the children, who are peeking past Henry at the large mirrors. "Sorry, someone must have told me wrong."

"No, no – come in," Henry says, standing aside for them to pass. The children free themselves from her grasp and rush to the barre. "No, let them," Henry says when she makes a half-hearted attempt to stop them. "They can't hurt anything." She is obviously a country woman, a coal miner's wife probably. "This was my mother's school, years ago," he tells her.

"People are saying her son is reopening the school," the woman says. "Are you her son?" Henry nods. "Well, I'd like to enroll my two." She nods in the direction of "her two," – a boy and a girl of very similar appearance. "Twins," she says. "I can pay. We're making good money at the moment." She means the mines are operating.

Henry is visited by equally compelling but opposite urges and makes his decision between them suddenly, without allowing himself to think. "Can you bring them twice a week? I don't know how long I'll be here, you know – I might be gone by this time next month, but I'll teach them while I'm here."

"In that case, can you make it three times a week, after school?" she asks, and he agrees. They decide upon the dates.

"May I ask you why you want them to learn so badly?" Henry asks her as they are leaving.

The woman sighs. "When I was a girl I saw ballet on TV, twice. I'll never forget it. I know it must be hard work." Her eyes inspect Henry beginning at his feet and ending at his eyes. "It is, isn't it?" Henry nods. "I would've given my eye teeth to do something like that – I would've worked night and day. I want them to have a taste of it. Even if it's only a taste, maybe it will make a difference to them, you know?"

"Yes, I know."

He watches through the window as she pushes the children into the car and drives away. Her parting words remain in his mind for a long time.

It seems the decision of whether or not to reopen the school has been made for him.

The fact that the high school where Pete teaches resumes classes again in three days is not the reason Pete fails to appear that day. So long as he is in Henry's presence, he is able to forget everything else, but when he is elsewhere, the weight of his dilemma threatens to break him. He comes to Henry out of weakness, because he cannot contemplate solutions to the problems he's created, but he knows he must find the will to forego Henry's company at least long enough to think things through. He spends a great deal of time in his darkroom in the basement working on the photographs of Henry; they represent to him a kind of half-way point between their joint dream-world and his own real world, so that they might be a means of weaning himself from his dangerous vice. The fact that the development and perfection of photographs are so technical gives him a blessedly unemotional focus.

His dangerous vice is not sex. Pete cares equally little about sex with men or with women and makes no judgments of others or of himself on the basis of sexual behavior. His vice is that he is enamored of what Henry stands for: the freedom to leave; the freedom to answer to oneself rather than to everybody else; the freedom to make art and beauty ones priorities, the capacity to direct his emotion through his art. To be with Henry is to be within that magical circle, that fairy ring where art and beauty live. To be outside it is to be bereft.

The photographs of Henry are the best work he's ever done, and the care he has lavished on the prints is worthy of the quality of the images themselves. He has photographed Henry in every conceivable way, from every angle and in every pose, dancing and resting, smiling and sober, from a distance and so close up that he would be unrecognizable as Henry to anyone but Pete. Linda was right to suggest he do this; his eye for inanimate form and its corresponding propensity for coldness is mitigated by the human subject – both the humanity and the inanimate line are heightened in the process. He tries not to think about the irony that it was Linda's suggestion.

But to whom is he going to show these pictures? They are private. They shouldn't be – they are the one body of work he's done that he knows beyond doubt is fine, but his intimacy with Henry relegates them to the closet or the trash bin. Whoever sees them will know that Pete isn't who he has always shown himself to be. They will believe he is a fraud. He knows he isn't that, but he is a coward. The little world he shares with Henry is only a dream, a Utopia doomed to fail. Deep River is where he belongs, is the only place he has courage for, but when he looks at these photographs his heart swells with pride and disbelief that they are his. He doesn't know what to do.

He is staring at the last print he made, a detail of Henry's torso from the right side, with his left hand stretched dramatically toward the camera, the mirror behind him creating a hazy, ominous-looking background. He had been doing some sort of turn. It is a study in contrast, and Pete is thinking how odd it is that he uses even the human body as a means of abstract design, whereas Henry's use of it, through the dancer's necessary presence, is absolutely concrete. While his mind wanders along those lines, the phone rings. He drops the picture on the table and takes the basement stairs two at a time, because only Henry is in his mind.

"Mr. Pete?"

It takes Pete a moment, although there is only one person it can be. "Roy? Where are you?" They have never spoken together on the telephone before.

"I'm in Staunton. I've been here these two months – I found her, but she's been in the hospital. It's a long story – I'll tell you that some other time, when we're not on long distance. They let her out a few days ago."

"Well, thank God, Roy – you can bring her home then." There is silence on the other end, broken by a crackling in the wires, and even though Pete can read in that silence the whole demeaning purpose behind Roy's call, he asks, "Can't you?" And is sorry, because it only makes it harder for Roy. Quickly he tries to compensate. "Listen, Roy, whatever it is you need, I'll do. Don't worry. I'd ask you for help if I needed it." Would he?

"I don't know exactly what I need, Mr. Pete. We're stuck in one room over here, and that's not good, but we'll be stuck in one room there too. " There is something else though, Pete is sure.

"Do you have money for the train?"

"It's not that. I got a little job here, but the truth is, I can't leave Sarah by herself, even to go to work."

"Look, Roy, I'm going to come over and get you – no arguments. Tell me how to get there. Then we'll sort it out."

It is three o'clock when he leaves – the drive to Staunton will take him four hours, so he can be there before dark if he doesn't dally.

He's half way there before he remembers that Henry would be expecting him.

Oddly enough, Henry has never been to Pete's house. He parks at the foot of the hill and walks up the stone stairs below the retaining wall and along the path past Roy's cottage, where he lingers for a few minutes, trying to sniff out a sense of the deserted place's character. He likes it; it reminds him of places he's read about in books that were written a century earlier, fieldstone, humble, well-cared-for, and lived-in. He walks on past it, to Pete's house, further along the hill. The drivable road snakes up behind it, but there is no car parked there. The house itself is a two-storey frame dwelling with drop siding painted white and stacked porches on the front, the top one screened-in. It too has a comfortable, yesteryear feel, which doesn't surprise Henry, but it isn't quite as well tended as Roy's place and that does surprise him. The effort has been made, but there is simply too much for one person to take care of. Retaining walls are everywhere, beautiful walls built exactly where they are needed, out of the local stone that litters every acre of the land. They are obviously Roy's work – their construction matches that of Roy's house, the walls adjoining it, and the wall behind Bella's house. He wonders if every wall in the valley is Roy's doing. Above the ones around Pete's house all sorts of things had been planted in the spring, but not tended. Some of them have run riot while others have been squeezed out by wild vines and weeds. Henry suspects that Roy's departure coincided with the first failure of attention to the well-planned gardens.

He tries the back door and finds it unlocked, so he lets himself in thinking he will leave Pete a note. He doesn't want to snoop, but he can't help taking a look at the downstairs. It doesn't remind him of Pete. The cheap fifties furniture is worn and scratched, the shelves of a corner cupboard and the living room side tables are adorned with family photographs and knick-knacks that Henry can't imagine Pete even noticing. The only real evidence of Pete's personality is on the dining room table, where he has piled schoolbooks for his classes (*The Oxford Anthology of American Verse, The Oxford Anthology of English verse, The Fire Next Time, Silas Marner, Macbeth*) and photographic equipment. Henry finds a pencil and paper, writes a brief note and leaves it on the kitchen counter.

When he walks back past Roy's, his eye lights on the unused workbench with its two grinding stones set in the edge. Something in the very back of his brain stirs, a fragment of memory, a man's voice from far away. But it can't possibly have anything to do with this place – he was already gone before Roy built his house on this spot.

He shrugs it off and goes home to Bella.

"She's pretty weak this evening, Henry." Pat, the other nurse is sitting at the kitchen table with a cup of coffee when he comes in. Henry, like Bella, prefers her to Mary – she is more restful. Henry sits down at the table. "You look tired," Pat observes and without asking gets up and pours him coffee, puts the sugar bowl on the table.

He laughs and pulls the coffee cup close. "Haven't had enough caffeine today, that's all."

"Someone called for you this afternoon." She pulls a slip of paper out of her dress pocket and gives it to him. "He sounded peeved not to talk to you."

Henry looks at the paper. Hector. "My boss," he says. "He always sounds peeved. I'll call him tonight."

"Well, I'll be going," she says but stands for a moment looking at him critically. "If you don't mind my saying so, this is going to wear you out if you're not careful. You should get someone in at night."

"Linda Paisley's going to look into it for me," he says. "Every other night will be enough."

She thinks it over. "If it's every other night, I could do it for you – just stay on the days I come anyway. We could use the extra money; besides, I like your mother, and she likes me."

Henry smiles up at her, unaware of the smudgy shadows under his eyes. "I know she does. If you really don't mind, that would be better than another new person. But what about your family?"

She shrugs. "He'll be happier to see the money than to see me. So – I'll start day after tomorrow?"

"Sure. Perfect. I'll call Linda and tell her to call off the search."

After Pat leaves, he telephones Linda, then stares at the note with Hector's name and number but decides to wait until later to call him. He goes upstairs and into Bella's room, where a warm breeze teases at the curtains and the air feels and smells stuffy. It is hotter upstairs than down, but Bella is under two blankets. Her skin has a sticky look to it, so he puts his hand to her head to see if she is hot. She opens her eyes. "Hot tonight, isn't it?" she asks rhetorically. "But I can't really tell – I'm either sweating or shivering and I don't think it's because of the weather. Leave the covers alone – if you take them off I'll just ant them again in five minutes."

They have never asked each other questions like "How are you?" or "How was your day?" and the recent revelations they have had about each other haven't changed that. Henry pulls the little Victorian rocker close to the bed and sits in it, throwing his head back against the wooden rim. He rocks a little. Bella scoots her body right to the edge of the bed, lying on her side, so that she

165

can be as close as possible to him. She pushes the pillow away and lays her cheek on her hand instead.

"Your Uncle Adrian was at Jesus College, the same one that Lawrence of Arabia was in, but of course not at the same time" Bella says out of the blue.

"What brought that to mind?"

"Well, lying here all day, my mind roams over a fairly wide territory. Your father admired Lawrence greatly."

"I know. The *Seven Pillars* downstairs is one of the few books I haven't read."

"You should. It's extraordinary, as a piece of literature if nothing else. It's the one book that – well, it's one of his books. You had been asking about my family. Max rather admired English things in general, hence his attraction to me, but Lawrence – whom he'd learned of as a boy reading Lowell Thomas – came to mean much more because of the war. Max never talked about his experiences in the war, but he came back changed – and decorated. At least, I thought he had changed, although I hadn't known him at all well before. We'd only just met, through my brother."

"Did you have theories about the difference in him?"

"The same theory everyone had. It happened to

many men, and the Ardennes Offensive was, by all reports, terrible. I don't know what he saw, or did. I always wondered if he felt guilty for something, but they say that's normal too. He never told me much, Henry. I doubt he told anyone very much."

She lies on her side speaking softly, and Henry is aware that the quality of her speech has changed since he's been home. Over the years, her genteel English accent had become muted by her environment and corrupted by her own increasing boredom with what she had to say. She had come to express herself in brief, scraping bursts of biting words that said so little that Henry had not actually felt compelled to listen. Now, it is not only her words that hold meaning, but also her voice; speech is bringing the past forward as much as thought, and the sound of it is pleasing – Henry wishes she would talk and talk.

"That must have been lonely – for both of you," Henry says after a moment. It is the first thought that her words evoke, and with it a clear picture of his two parents, unable to bridge the space between them. His perception comes as a surprise to Bella, who takes a deep breath and pushes her thoughts to other territory. This one might lead to revelations she has sworn not to indulge in. "I wish you would tell me more about Max," Henry says finally, and that is when Bella feigns sleep. He leaves the room to make his call to Hector, but she hasn't fooled him. He knows now with certainty that she has things to tell.

He goes back downstairs to make the phone call on the old wall phone in the kitchen, which has a long cord. He sits at the table and props his bare feet up on it, running his fingers in and out of the coiled wire, and pointing and flexing his feet out of habit. Hector picks up on the second ring, and Henry hears other voices in the background. Some sort of party. He has a sudden, brief but engulfing nostalgia for the city; it is like smelling the burnt chestnuts the street vendors sell.

"Hector, it's Henry."

"Henry! Wait a second." The phone drops and a minute later the voices are cut off. "There are a lot of people here, sorry. I've gone in the bedroom. How's your mother?"

'Not so good. She was holding steady there for awhile, but not now. She's very week."

A silence. "I'm sorry," Hector says finally. "Are you holding up okay?"

"Oh, sure. I've hired a couple of women to help. I've reopened my mother's school, can you believe it? As of today I have two eight year old students, a boy and a girl. Amazing - fifty percent of my students are boys. They're twins." He stops, aware of an uncharacteristic patience on the other end. "I'm fine, Hector."

"Well. All right. I want to talk to you about the

fall season, Henry, just so we're clear about this. You won't be dancing – that suits both of us, right?"

Of course. "Right," Henry says.

"I assume you're working out. How's your knee?"

"Not bad, actually, but I don't know how it would be under real duress."

"Okay, here's what I suggest. You do – what you're doing there, and forget about touring this winter. But, Henry, think about having the surgery, so you can get through therapy in time for me to reinstate you before next year's summer season here. How's that sound?"

It sounds like a long, empty winter, is how it sounds, but what choice do either of them have? "It's good, Hector. I – no, it's good. Thanks."

"There's something else."

"What?"

Hector's voice is amused. "Don't sound so edgy. Simon Bowles has been trying to get hold of you."

"Simon Bowles?" Simon Bowles, a recently retired dancer of legendary stature, is the artistic director of a new English company currently being talked about. Henry hears something that sounds like a chuckle.

"As a matter of fact, he's here tonight. Let me go

get him."

Henry has never met Simon Bowles, but he has seen him dance – a handsome blond Englishman. He is now forty-two, having been in his prime when Henry was starting out. He is known as someone with a sixth sense about taking risks. Henry's pulse has quickened just a little, a feeling he hasn't experienced in quite some time.

"Hello?"

"Mr. Bowles? This is Henry Oliver."

Henry hears the other man say something indistinguishable, then Hector's responding laugh.

"Hector didn't tell me you were on the line. Hello, Henry. Not the best time to talk – it's a madhouse here."

"What else is new?"

"Well, my company's in town. You didn't know? It's going very well. Very well indeed. Hector is throwing a little dinner party for me tonight - about thirty people. Now, down to business – did Hector say anything?"

"He said you were trying to get hold of me."

"Yes, well, more-or-less. I knew you were out of town – everyone knows. Hector was afraid I would try to steal you away – take you back to London. If I thought I could, I would, of course. He was relieved when I told him I only want to commission a work. Would that fit in with your plans at all?"

"What can I say, Mr. Bowles? It would be thrilling."

"Don't call me Mr. Bowles – I'm not *that* old. Call me Simon, please. We're colleagues. I've seen you dance, and I saw both *Songs and Ayres* and *Dowland Dances*. More than once. Very impressive."

"Thank you."

"We can't talk now. Can I call you, where you are? Good – I'll get the number from Hector. 'Bye."

Henry sat for ten minutes holding the receiver and staring at it with his mouth hanging open, unaware even of the recorded voice when it came on telling him to hang up. Where is all his disdain for his old ballet life now, or is it just that he's thinking of running away again?

6. RELAPSES

It is just getting dark when Pete arrives in Staunton. He has stopped only once for gas and a coke and would like more than anything a swim in a motel swimming pool, then a shower and a beer and hamburger. He goes first to Roy's. The street in which Roy and Sarah are staying is full of potholes and winds up a little hill through small single-family dwellings and old frame rooming houses, now called "apartment buildings" – it is to one of these that Roy has given him careful directions. He parks on the street and climbs the crumbling cement stairs from the street to the building and then to the second floor where he knocks on the door at the top of the stairs. He hears a familiar voice inside, and the door is flung open. The relief on Roy's face is unmistakable if mixed with some apprehension. Pete can't help it; he throws his arms around the other man wanting to reassure him that now everything will be all right. Roy lets him go ahead and think that he agrees.

"I'm mighty glad to see you, Pete. Come on in." Pete. So it had finally happened.

"You realize what you just did, called me just plain Pete? That means you can't go back, you understand. No more Mr., ever again."

Roy laughed. "Okay. I reckon your coming all the way over here puts us on some kind of different footing. I owe you the world for this."

Pete shook his head. "No, you don't. I was happy to do it. Not just for you, either. For myself. Now introduce me to Sarah." He is staring at the back of a fine boned woman with luxuriant black hair, standing at the window. Roy moves toward her and Pete follows him.

"Sary," Roy says, but she pays no attention until he touches her shoulder, which make her jump. "Look, Sary, I've told you about Pete, who lives next door to me – he's come to take us home." He speaks to her in tones one would use with a child, coaxing her to somehow believe in his words while knowing that she won't. She turns around though, her eyes dreamy from their unfocused attention to the world outside, and although she looks at Pete, he has the feeling that she doesn't see him. He holds out his hand to take hers, but she doesn't notice until Roy nudges her elbow. "Shake Pete's hand, honey."

"How do you do," Pete says, using formality to bridge the chasm between himself – between everyone – and this woman. But there is no bridge long enough, he can see that instantly. He knows now why Roy called him.

She is as unlike Roy as it is possible to be, fine-featured and light-skinned. She would be beautiful if she weren't so thin and used. Where has she been all these years? "With the hippies," is what people say at home, but there is no sense that she has ever experienced a summer of love. He thinks, then, uncomfortably, of his own situation and how quickly one's position can change. Not that change in itself is undesirable, except so often it controls one, instead of the other way around. Long ago, she must have gone out to meet life, thinking it was on her own terms, and become lost. It was so easy to do, Pete has come to realize in the past few months. It is so easy to do even when one doesn't go off deliberately courting adventure. How much greater the dangers must be to someone who does that. He shifts his eyes to Roy, who is staring at his daughter with a look halfway between fear and adoration. He understands now why Roy has never said much about her. What is there to say? Yet seeing her explains it all only raises more questions.

"I must have met you before, Sarah," he says, hoping that they can somehow relax into an ordinary pleasantness. "A long time ago – maybe when we were kids. You look awfully familiar." But his words don't help. Sarah ignores him, and the expression on Roy's face becomes more taut. "What time do you want to leave tomorrow, Roy?" The room is devoid of personal items; two suitcases sit half full on the visible single bed. Pete sees another bed behind the curtain draped across the center of the room.

"Any time, is fine. We'll be ready early, and I've already settled with the landlady."

They agree on 8 o'clock, and Pete leaves to find a motel, with a pool, a shower, a beer and a hamburger. When he does find it, he spends much longer than he intended in the pool, swimming mindless laps. He feels better after that and tries to stop thinking about Roy and Sarah – there will be plenty of time to do that tomorrow. It is hard, though. He keeps seeing her face and thin, hunched shoulders. He doesn't remember ever meeting her in childhood or any other time, but he's seen her before – it bothers him that he can't remember.

As he comes up the stairs to the apartment the following morning, he hears a woman's shouting voice. "You fuckin' idiot, Daddy – why did you come? I don't want to go back there – everyone will laugh at me. What will I do?" He hesitates outside the door listening to the softer tones of Roy's voice trying to sooth her. "No one's going to think anything, Sary. It's been a long, long time – too long. We'll just take it day by day, like we always used to, okay?"

"Not long enough, is more like it. I always hated that shithole; I never meant to go back, never." Her vulgarity is so at odds with her appearance that Pete is shocked in spite of himself.

Roy's voice is firmer this time. "Well you have to. The court says you have to be with me, and I need to go back there." Pleading. "You might like it now, honey. Find it peaceful." She is weeping, and Pete imagines that Roy

175

has put his arms around her. "There, there." He knocks.

The drive home is tense, so dominated by the woman's instability that no conversation is possible. Apologetically, Roy sits with her in the back seat and more than once must restrain her when she tries to open the door. Her behavior is completely unpredictable, one moment childlike and fragile, the next ugly and tough. About an hour before they start down the final mountain into the valley, she falls asleep with her head in Roy's lap.

"So now you see," Roy says.

"What will you do? You can't live with her in your house, Roy."

"You tell me what choice I have. I'll think of something."

"Maybe you'd both better come stay up at my house for now," Pete suggests. He knows beforehand what the reply will be and is uncomfortably aware that he might not have made the suggestion otherwise.

"No." Roy is firm on this point. "I appreciate the offer, but it wouldn't work. Best get used to things as they are." He is gently stroking her hair as he speaks. "She's never been easy. I was used to it, once. I'll get used to it again. Strange, to want nothing more than to make someone happy, and not be able to. A child, at that – back then. You'd think it'd be easy, wouldn't you?"

Pete doesn't know. An hour later, he pulls the car into the little grassy place below Roy's wall and lets them out. "No, don't come up, Pete. You want to get home, and we can manage. Come on, now Sary, we're there – just up the hill. It's small but it's nice." She stirs and sits up, groaning, and looks out the window. Pete watches her in the rear view mirror as she looks up toward the little house nestled into the hillside. It is still very green, but because of the heat and dryness, some leaves are beginning to wither and fall. What does she see? Pete wonders. Poverty, failure and a dead end? She hasn't found anything else where she has been. Observing, he believes he sees a small softening of her lips, as though her view of the pretty hillside where Roy lives is not the worst thing in the world. Still, he can't imagine how Roy is going to cope with this. The only positive thought he has about the situation is in reference to himself: he now has firsthand evidence that there are far worse predicaments than this own.

The first thing he sees when he lets himself into his own house is the note from Henry, and it is only then that he realizes he went off without letting anyone know. He looks up the number and reluctantly calls Bella's house. A woman he doesn't know answers, one of the caregivers, which means Henry has left to go to the studio. Pete doesn't want to go to the studio.

"Oh, no, he's still here," the woman says. "His mother isn't doing very well so he's stayed home. Who's calling?" A moment later Henry answers.

"Is Bella very bad?" Pete asks.

"I think so. Doc Roberts is here. Where have you been?" There is no reproach, not even much curiosity, and Pete feels suddenly embarrassed. He tells Henry about Roy and Sarah.

"That doesn't sound good," Henry says, but his tone is disinterested. The silence that ensues feels awkward to Pete although he thinks Henry hardly notices.

"Well, I better let you go," Pete says.

"Look, why don't you come up here? Bella would love to see you."

"Now?"

"If you can."

He puts some peanut butter on a piece of bread and eats it hurriedly then washes his hands and leaves. In spite of his fledgling resolve, he can't wait to see Henry. He has forgotten about everything else.

As always, the back door of Bella's is unlocked and Pete lets himself in. The comfortable but taciturn woman he had spoken to on the phone is sitting at the kitchen table eating her lunch and without rising from her seat introduces herself as Pat. "The doctor's left," she tells him. "Henry's upstairs – go on up."

His feet make no sound on the carpeted stairs, so he arrives at Bella's bedroom door unnoticed and stands outside the doorway. From there he can see most of the room: the covers on the spool bed are neatly spread over the still figure, the curtains flutter a little at the open window through which, Pete registers only fleetingly, the smell of smoke is detectable. And in the little rocker beside the bed, another motionless figure. He enters the room still unnoticed and it is only when he is a few feet away that he realizes Henry's eyes are closed. He puts his big hand on Henry's shoulder and Henry starts then relaxes, reaches up and squeezes Pete's hand before quickly releasing it. He moves out of the chair and to the bed to look down at his mother and then motions Pete to follow him into the hallway.

"Let's go downstairs," Henry whispers, and it seems to Pete that Henry is careful to avoid touching him. "I'll get Pat to come up. Bella will wake up soon, then you can visit."

In the kitchen the light is brighter and Pete can see the signs of fatigue in Henry. His eyes are red-rimmed and dark-circled, his skin looks both pinched and slack at once. Henry sees him looking and smiles. "I've been up all night." When Pat leaves the room, Pete takes her place at the table while Henry makes tea.

"Do you mind tea?" he asks as though he's talking to himself. "Bella will want tea in a bit, so I thought I'd make a pot." While the water is heating Henry sits down across from Pete and crosses his arms on the tabletop. He seems suddenly focused, and Pete is put in mind of other times when he's seen this sudden switch in Henry, a capacity for total mental discipline even when he is obviously exhausted.

"Pete, I went to see Linda the other day," he says without preamble. "She told me you had asked her to marry you."

Pete is looking at him when he begins to speak but the lack of emotion in his voice causes Pete to drop his eyes to his own hands laced together on the table. Pete's thoughts are suddenly irrelevant, childish – not thoughts but the immature faith that longing makes things happen, and that if you want something badly enough, the other person is going to want it too. But I don't even know what I want, Pete thinks, although that is not what upsets and embarrasses him about this encounter. What upsets and embarrasses him is that he has no idea what Henry is thinking, and he cannot bring himself to ask, which is surely a condemning reflection of their friendship. When he raises his eyes, Henry is watching him.

"Yes, I did. I....I don't see what business it is of yours." He stops. What is he supposed to say? That he's changed his mind because he prefers Henry's company, prefers his frame of mind, his conversation, his laughter, and –yes– his body? That is what he has thought these past two months, but now seeing how silly it must be to someone as worldly as Henry, he is ashamed. He doesn't actually know what Henry's frame of mind is, except about fitting dance to music or about certain books they have both read. Do those things necessarily indicate a frame of mind? How many people Henry must know with whom he actually does share his mind and whose conversation is on a par with his own. How many beautiful men – and women too, for all Pete knows – must have felt about Henry's body the way Pete does, and perhaps had the feeling reciprocated. Given these questions, nothing Pete has thought about their friendship rings true even to himself. They have shared very little about their lives, Henry even less than Pete. He probably feels that Pete wouldn't understand his sophisticated world.

His embarrassed silence lasts so long that Henry, watching, decides he has approached this the wrong way. "It's just that I'm worried about Linda, Pete. She doesn't understand why you don't come around more often. You must think about that sometimes. Are you staying away on account of me?" There is an understated incredulity in his tone.

Henry has removed his own hands from the tabletop so that they can clench and unclench unseen against his knees. He hates this. He has wandered into this strange friendship willingly and, without his usual self-discipline has allowed it to stray into the physical, a mistake in this case – he and Pete are not on equal turf. Pete is not entirely a romantic, but he clings still to the old domestic model: love and commitment.

"What do you think?" Pete asks in response to Henry's question, and it is almost a sneer. He starts to rise. "I'd better go."

"No, sit down. I'm sorry, if you've somehow been mislead. I'm very fond of you. But I keep my physical and emotional – activities - entirely separate."

"As far as I can see, you don't have any emotional activities, besides your work." Pete says, sitting back down. "You haven't mislead me – I knew that about you before. I've mislead myself, let myself get off-course. I'm afraid to be around Linda just now. I'm too transparent, but I don't want her to know what's gone on between you and me."

"Do you think she wouldn't understand?"

"She would be kind and give me her rational understanding but hide whatever was going on for herself, inside. That's what we all do around here – either that, or because of our feelings of impotence get drunk and beat our wives and children, if we have any. Everybody knows that about Appalachia, remember?"

"Stop being sarcastic. It doesn't suit you." Oddly, Pete comes close to tears of gratitude at Henry's words.

Although critical, they are the first truly personal response Henry has given him.

"How do you know what suits me? And I'm not being sarcastic," Pete says. "You're bound to have seen it. It's a sort of conspiracy of goodness, lies for the common good. Only who really knows what the common good is? It's like watching Roy this morning, struggling to convince me and Sarah and himself that everything can be okay at some unknown date in the future, when the opposite is so obviously true. God, there's a history there! But who can get to it now, after all the years of pretense? We've all worked so hard at hiding the unpleasant truths from each other that no one knows what's going on anymore."

"You're doing, right now, what you accuse Linda and everyone else of. Why not just tell her about your…"

"…my attachment to you."

"Okay, your attachment to me and see what happens? At least then you wouldn't be hiding anything."

This time Pete does get up from his seat. "You really are cold at heart, aren't you?"

Unperturbed Henry remains in his seat and stares up at his friend. "Absolutely. And you can't leave – you have to go up and see Bella."

Henry forces himself to meet Pete's hurt and

condemning eye just before Pete turns to go upstairs. Alone again, he replaces his hands on the table where he can see them, as though he is afraid they might do something on their own otherwise.

"You really are cold at heart, aren't you?" Absolutely. It is the only way to be, when your friends are hurting and your mother is dying, and you can't move forward and you don't want to go back, and you are running in place in a place that you can't escape because you've never decided whether you really want to escape or not. God, I am so tired, he thinks. In order to avoid Pete when he comes down, he goes out the back door and up the hill to his old spot, where the dead leaves have already covered the mossy ground. He sits for awhile on the stone slab, vaguely worried about snakes, thinking of nothing in particular, until even to one in his deliberately vacant state of mind the heavy smell of smoke becomes unavoidable. Reluctantly he gets to his feet and pulls the vines away for a better view. Across the river, on not one but three of the wooded hillsides, bright flame eats its ragged way through the scenery, edging downward from the summit toward the fragile miniature townships at the base of the mountain. How appropriate. He almost laughs.

Pat is putting something in the linen closet in the hall when Pete goes up. She smiles at him. "Mrs. Oliver's awake. I'm sure she'll be happy for some new company."

Pete enters Bella's room. She is lying on her back but her head is turned toward the empty rocking chair. Silently he walks around the bed until he is standing in front of the chair, and he can see by her smile – all mischief not quite fled – that she has known all along he was there. She holds up her hand for him to take, and he sits on the edge of the bed where he can hold it easily and look at her. Her small hand, between his two big ones, feels soft and dry – not at all unhealthy. He lays it flat on his palm and holds it so he can look at it, and is startled by its resemblance to the long slender hand of her son. He tells her so. "Henry has long fingers like yours."

"It's funny, isn't it? For all his tall leanness, Max had short, rather ugly hands. When Henry was made, it was with all the best materials from each of his parents."

"Physically, you mean." Pete avoids her astute gaze.

"No, not just," she replies. Then, cautiously: "Henry doesn't always show his true intentions, I think. I wonder sometimes if he knows what they are. I used to think…"

"What?"

"Oh, I don't know. How are you, Pete? You're looking a little bothered."

"Tired, I guess. I drove to Staunton yesterday, to get Roy and Sarah. We returned this morning. It wasn't the drive so much as the tension. Sarah is a mess – she just got out of drug rehab. She's nothing like Roy – one minute she acts as though she's five years old and the next she's as vulgar and unpleasant as anyone I've ever met, a little scary. She must have been very pretty before the drugs did their work. I don't remember it at all, but we must have met as children – she looks very familiar. I don't know what he's going to do with her – he won't accept much help."

"Well, this is something he's got to figure out for himself, don't you think? He always spoiled her. And she's a grown woman, not a girl any longer – he's an old man. She should be taking care of him, not the other way around."

Pete looks at her curiously but says, "Its strange that someone like Roy would have a daughter like Sarah – her character so unlike his, her looks – her skin is very light."

"No, Sarah's not Roy's daughter."

"Yes, she is."

"No," Bella insists. "She's his niece, his sister's child."

"Are you sure?"

"Oh yes. Although there's no reason why you should know that – you're too young. She's older than Henry."

"Why should he have kept it secret?"

"Not exactly secret, but for the girl's sake perhaps it

186

wasn't advertised." She looks toward the window and changes the subject. "My olfactory sense is none too good these days – do I smell smoke?"

Pete stands and walks to the window. "The forest fire season has started," he says, a little alarmed. There are always forest fires in the fall, usually small and questionably harmful, but this fall is abnormally dry. He turns back toward Bella, and sees then that their talk has tired her.

"I'd better go," he says, bending over to kiss her. She puts her hand on his shoulder and holds him there for a moment.

"Two favors," she whispers. "Get Henry out of his own mind from time to time if you can, okay? Don't ask me how – I've never known."

What is he to say? He nods and asks, "And the other favor?"

"Tell Roy I want him to come see me. Tell him…tell him I would be pleased – no – *honored*, if he would come see me. He can bring the girl too if he wants."

She is extremely fond of Pete and enjoys his visit but is relieved when he leaves – seeing people requires energy, of which she has very little. She doesn't mind Pat, who comes and goes quietly or sits in the rocker and knits, as lost in her thoughts as Bella is in her own. As for Henry – the change between them, unspoken but mutually acknowledged, is partly a longing to be in proximity to each other before it is too late. But perhaps that isn't a new longing, only newly recognized. He often sits in the rocking chair most of the night, and when she opens her eyes, as she does every few minutes, and the dim light of the little lamp they keep burning illuminates the tips of his hair, the planes of his face, the shapely lips softened in fatigue, tears inevitably fill her eyes. She doesn't mind them, because it is a new sensation. She just lies there in the silence watching him the way one might study a Rembrandt painting, which is a little what the lighting reminds her of.

Often, she floats in the state between sleeping and waking where dreams are most real. The dreams come unbidden, always nowadays some fragment of the past, and she is eager for them, to see what they contain and if she can discover anything new of the original events that she hadn't discovered long ago. She hasn't much time. If she is ever to understand, it has to be now.

The dream she inhabits after Pete leaves is of the day she described for Max Henry's behavior at dance class. She did that on a Monday, after the fourth class, after it became clear to her that Henry's interest was unusual. The classes were Monday, Wednesday and Friday. Later, she expanded to Saturday as well.

She put Henry in the bathtub when they got home. "Think you can manage by yourself?" she asked.

"Yes, I can manage, Mama," he said seriously, holding onto his toes while his oddly adult gray eyes looked up at her from the water. She laid his towel with his pajamas on the shut toilet seat.

"Then I'll go fix us some supper. Clean everywhere, now, and don't slip when you get out." He nodded.

Later, when she put him to bed, he was still excited. "I wish the classes were every day. I wish we could go tomorrow."

"You like dancing very much, don't you? I did too, when I was your age. I never wanted to do anything else, except read books – I liked that too."

"Yes, very much, Mama, and I like books, too."

"Sleep, now." She kissed his forehead. "Perhaps you'll dream that you are dancing, and it will be even better than the real thing because you'll be as good as if you'd been practicing for years, instead of just one week."

"One day, I'll practice for years," he said sleepily. "I'll be so good. You and Papa will be proud of me."

"We're proud of you now, darling boy." She didn't sing to him. She didn't have much of a voice nor was she the singing sort of mother. She hadn't been sung to as a child either.

Max came home at eight, when she was in the kitchen cleaning up and wondering whether to take his dinner out of the oven and put it in the refrigerator. She was at the sink and didn't hear him because the water was running. He put his arm around her briefly and bit her ear. "Hello, darling." Dahling, he said, mimicking her accent – his doing so had once been in genuine fun; now she knew that he was mocking both of them. Her ear stung where he had bitten it, but she ignored it, turned her head a little to reach his cheek with her lips, but he had already released her and gone to the refrigerator. She turned off the water.

"Are you hungry? There's a fricassee in the oven." One of the few things she never ruined.

"I am, as a matter of fact," he said, dumping ice in a glass and reaching under the sink for the bourbon. He held it up. "Join me?"

"No thanks. I had a glass of sherry before Henry and I ate our supper."

"He's in bed?"

"Just. He's probably still awake, if you want to go up." He didn't respond to the suggestion but carried his glass to the table and sat while she took the stew out of the oven and brought it to the table. After she had served him, she sat down in the chair across from his.

"Good day?" she asked.

"Hmmm," he said, forking a piece of chicken into his mouth. "Busy. The VIPs are coming down from New York next week. Trying to get everything in order for them." They sat in silence while he ate. It had been years since they had found conversation easy. Bella had never learned to gauge her words according to whether or not they would irritate him and cause him to lash out. He preferred silence, but, eventually, he was the one who broke it.

"You had your little class today, didn't you? How did it go?"

"Fine. Very well, in fact. I have eleven students already – two more than last week. Imagine!"

Max raised his eyebrows. "At this rate, you'll have to hire more teachers. Henry bored out of his skull yet? Don't have to stand him in the corner?"

"Not at all." She hesitated. "Not at all. In fact, he's taking the class too. So actually I have twelve students, don't I? Mes éleves." She knew the French would annoy him.

Max put down his fork. "What do you mean?"

She forged ahead, already convinced she'd made a mistake in telling him, but she wanted him to know, so badly. "Last Monday, he stood behind all the little girls and did what they did – I didn't even notice till the end. The girls thought it very cute. On Wednesday, he moved up in front of them all, so he could see. So now he has his own place at the barre and does everything the girls do, only better. Imagine, Max. Perhaps he'll make a dancer."

Max grimaced sarcastically. "Like his mother? Really, Bella – he's a boy. No son of mine is going to be a ballet dancer. He'll tire of it soon; then you'll have to figure something out."

She knew already that he was wrong, although she didn't say so. Still, she wasn't going to back down, this time. "There'd be nothing wrong with it if he wanted to be a dancer. They're the best athletes in the world. I'd be proud, if you weren't. But he's just a little boy – don't discourage him, please, Max. Let him enjoy it. He's so happy."

Max shoved his plate away and pushed his chair back. "I've no intention of interfering, one way or the other unless it proves to be a problem. He can do it for a year or so – after that, the other children will tease him mercilessly – he'll have to quit." Max sighed and stood. "I don't even know why we're discussing this, Bella – we both know his interest won't last. Things get so complicated with you sometimes. I'm going to go read."

She sat at the table until she heard him go up, thinking about the school, the girls, Henry, and Max. As many times as she had tried to tell Max, he still had no idea of what Henry was like – that even at five years old, he didn't give up on things, or lose interest. Max didn't see it because he didn't want to see it, but why didn't he want to see it? He often seemed to fling Henry at her as a kind of reproach, and then he could use expressions like "no son of mine is going to be a ballet dancer." As though Henry were a commodity, the bought child. As she sometimes felt she was the bought wife.

Yet just when she had given up hope and retreated to a state of mind from which she thought she could cope with Max's disdain, he would change. That day had been a good example.

She waited for another half hour after he had gone upstairs, to allow him time to settle and fall asleep so she wouldn't disturb him. Then she turned off the downstairs lights and went up, washed her face in the bathroom across the hall, undressed and put on her nightgown. She heard his regular breathing as she crossed the room and crawled into her side of the bed, sure he was asleep. But when she had pulled the covers around herself and curled on her side with her back to him, she felt his arms come around her and his breath on her neck, and his teeth again – this time tenderly – on her ear.

"Thought you'd sneak in unnoticed, did you

darling?" This time there was no mockery in his tone. His tongue was in her ear and his hands pulling on her nightdress, and she tried to turn toward him, but he wouldn't let her. This way, when he had her caught and helpless but with her back to him, his tenderness nearly undid them both; he whispered and meant every known endearment while his touch ranged the repertoire of lovers until they were both sobbing, broken by their need and love for each other. Then, after, in the dark, he would turn her head into his shoulder and hold her while they lay exhausted and content, whispering about silly, happy things. That night, he said, "I looked in on Henry. He's a pretty little thing, isn't he?"

"Of course. He looks exactly like you."

Max chuckled. "A ballet dancer, eh? Could be worse, I guess. Let's see what Deep River makes of it! I love you, Bella."

This was how he did it, broke her resolve and kept her in thrall. It was only in the daytime and face to face that he couldn't stand the sight of her.

Guiltily Pete avoids Roy's cottage on the way home and drives to his own house via the back road. Bella's parting words remain in his mind, but his brain can't manage to coordinate her wish to see Roy with his recent experience driving them back from Staunton. And then there is her request to him concerning Henry, following so soon after he had reached his own more negative conclusion regarding Henry's supposed self-containment. He doesn't want to think about any of it. He will collect himself and deliver her message to Roy later, and as for Henry, well, he will have to sleep on that. The distance between them now, it seems to him, is insurmountable and he can hardly bear it. He is going to have a beer, or perhaps two. Or three.

The phone is ringing when he enters the kitchen. It is John Daley, his pilot and forestry service friend.

"Wanna go flying tomorrow, Pete? I've been asked to check the fires, take a tally you might say. You'd mentioned wanting to take pictures – I thought this might be a good opportunity, and I'd enjoy the company."

It takes Pete by surprise, so that he doesn't have time to formulate the excuse necessary to camouflage his fear of flying. He has been in an airplane exactly once: when he flew to New York for Mary Kay's graduation. He had canceled his return flight and taken the train. It is a fear he is embarrassed by, however. He doesn't give himself a moment to think. "Sure, that sounds good. What time tomorrow?"

"First thing in the morning. Can you be at the airport at eight?"

"I'll be there," he hears his hearty, false self say.

He takes a beer from the refrigerator, drinks it quickly, takes another one and carries it downstairs to the basement, where all the beautiful photographs of Henry are still stacked on the worktable. He doesn't want to look at them, ever, but he lacks the violence to destroy them, so he merely sweeps them up and dumps them in the empty trashcan at the end of the table. Then he goes upstairs again, takes his third beer from the refrigerator, and calls the one person to whom he can confess his apprehensions about flying.

Linda suggests that he come down and eat supper with them and then changes her mind. "How many beers have you had?" she asks.

"Almost done with my third. I don't really want to see Ruthie, Linda, much as I like her."

Even the three beers haven't affected Pete so much that he fails to detect the caution in her tone. "Do you want me to come up?"

"Would you?"

"Let me tell Ruthie. I should be there in half an hour."

Pete doesn't finish the third beer but sets the bottle on the edge of the sink and returns to the basement to get the equipment he will need for tomorrow.

Lately Linda has wondered if something is in the air driving people apart. She has noticed before how unreliable intimacy is – any sort of intimacy – and how often almost everyone one knows seems to be afflicted simultaneously. Although you may feel close to your daughter, brother, parent, friend or lover one day, and secure in the knowledge that you may depend on that other person and he on you, the next day might bring a distance that seems unbridgeable and for no very compelling reason. Or perhaps it's just that, humans made as they are, there is no very compelling reason for such closeness in the first place. She has all sorts of examples in her own life and is well aware that she is not unusual. Ruthie's father, for instance – a man, boy really, she slept with exactly once. The boy himself was nothing to her a week later, but even now when she recalls that single evening's gentle innocence it makes her smile. And it resulted in Ruthie, the great accomplishment of her life. Jack was the only person to whom she ever revealed the father's identity – but one day soon she knows she will have to tell Ruthie, and explain to her how the reasons for her not knowing him were petty, not important, reasons.

After thinking about it, she had decided she would marry Pete, but then this unexplained distance ensued, reminding her that even if they regain their former comfort with each other they will lose it again. People do. She is lonely. She knows that he is too, but it would be worse to be together and be lonely. So she is philosophical as she drives toward Pete's house, relieved and cautious both.

She decides to park in the pull-off below Roy's house and walk. Even though the air smells of the burning trees across the river, the weather isn't quite as hot as it's been, so perhaps they will get a reprieve from the withering heat after all. It's September now – they are due for one, although what they really need is rain.

As she nears Roy's cottage, she hears voices – a woman's raised voice and a quieter one, male. Unaware of Pete's trip to Staunton and Roy's return, her first thought is that someone is up to mischief in Roy's house. She knocks on the door and immediately hears footsteps crossing the room, then the door is opened just enough for her to see who it is.

"Roy! You're back. I didn't know." Recognizing her, he opens it wider and then stands there, as unsure now of what to do as she is.

"Linda. Yes, Pete brought us back this afternoon."

"Pete?" She looks past him and sees the woman's figure in the shadows beside the bed. "You found Sarah then. Is everything all right?"

Roy glances toward Sarah, makes a decision, and steps toward Linda so that he is standing on the doorsill. He looks distraught. "The thing is she's cut herself, Linda, but I can't leave to get help, and I've got no phone or car. I don't know what to do." Now that he is in the light, she can see his distress, and his fatigue.

"Is it bad?"

"I think it might need a stitch or two. I've wrapped it up. I don't want to bother Pete again."

"Nonsense. I'm on my way there now. He's expecting me, so let me go tell him, and then I'll take her to the hospital. I'll be back in a few minutes."

As she hurries up the path she wonders how the girl cut herself. The girl. She must be close to her own age, but she still pictures her as the pretty, high –strung child she remembers from Sunday School. She knows nothing about her beyond the ten-year-old gossip, but it is odd that Roy had chosen not to introduce her.

Pete is sitting in the lazy-boy chair in the living room, half asleep, but he wakes up the moment she comes in. She is relieved to see that he isn't drunk, as she had half-expected him to be.

"I'm afraid I can't stay," she says, accepting his hesitant embrace. "I came up the path and saw Roy. Sarah has done something to herself and needs to go to the hospital. I said I would take her."

"I'll come with you."

They walk back to Roy's and in the few minutes it takes Pete tells her about his trip to Staunton and what he saw of Sarah's condition. "The situation seems impossible," he admits. "He spends all those years hunting for her, and now I wonder if he regrets having found her."

"Of course he doesn't," Linda says brusquely. "Is that what a white father would think?" But she says no more, thinking of how her own parents, so proud of their paler skin and wanting so badly to be thought of as white, had treated both her brother and herself because of their transgressions.

"I went to see Bella Oliver today. She says Sarah's not Roy's daughter, only his niece."

"That's interesting." She looks at him sharply. "You've been around today, haven't you?"

He laughs. "That's not the half of it. I'm supposed to go flying with John Daley in the morning. I'm terrified." It is a relief just to have said it and her response makes him feel much less foolish.

"I don't blame you. John Daley is a maniac," she says, rolling her eyes. "But you'll take some nice pictures." That is the thing he needs to hear, and it lightens the air between them.

It is Saturday evening and the emergency room is

busy, although less so than it will be later, when drunk teenagers with new driver's licenses are brought in. Sarah sits quietly, cradling the cut hand in the palm of her other hand, with Roy's arm around her. Linda and Pete sit in the opposite bank of waiting room chairs, each of them wondering what it feels like after so long a time to be together again. When Sarah is called Roy is allowed to go with her, and Linda and Pete finally have a chance to talk.

"How did it happen?" Pete asks, referring to Sarah's cut.

"I don't know," Linda tells him. "She's not all there really, is she? There were rumors, long ago, that she was touched."

"She was on heroin when Roy caught up with her – who knows for how long?"

They sit in silence for a while then both speak at once.

"Why didn't you call and tell me you were going...?"

"I'm sorry I've been so remote lately, Linda..." She lets him finish. "I guess I've had cold feet." It is such a cowardly interpretation of the truth that Pete colors.

"I guess the question is – are you going to stay remote?"

"I hope not. I don't plan to, at least – if that's okay with you."

"You asked me a question a couple of months ago, and I'd been all set to answer it. Now, I think I need more time again – unless you've retracted the question."

A hesitation. "No, I haven't. That's all right if you want more time," Pete says. "Of course I understand." He tries to make it sound as though he accepts what she says as his just recompense, but she reads him correctly, knows that he is glad for the reprieve. So as they sit and wait for Roy and Sarah, Linda is recalling her earlier thoughts about loneliness and human unreliability, while Pete, believing he has stalled successfully, has shifted his nervous attention to tomorrow's adventure.

7. IN THE ATTIC

Pat isn't a talkative woman, but she is a compassionate one, and she notices things about people. In the years that she has been sitting with the dying, listening to their thoughts, tending to their physical needs, she has learned that everyone has volumes and volumes of stories stored away, a library upon which they draw in those final weeks. She used to think that life was for childhood, for most children find ways to be content – they don't dream of the horrors to come. But she has grown to believe that almost everyone is granted some kind of revelation of herself in the end – one that makes both life and death seem better than they are. It is the middle part, the part everyone places the most value on, that - in personal terms at least – is always the failure. Even the very old, who hardly seem to have a wit left in their heads, appear to tap into a store of knowledge richer than anything she's ever known herself.

This household is more interesting than most. People talk about the son because he went away, and because he's a dancer, and because he's a little famous, but he is far more complicated than any of those definitions of him indicate. There is that other rumor too, of course, but she doesn't care one way or another about his sex life. She has had to study him very hard, in order to dispel for herself the things she has heard other people say, which are meaningless. He is very smart, that is obvious. And she can see why he might be a good dancer, for he is built like a cat. Her assessment is that he thinks too much. Even when he believes he is not thinking, as for instance when he has two or three glasses of wine around dinnertime, something she knows for a fact he did not do a month earlier. Even then, he thinks too much. She has grown to like him. His taciturnity matches hers. And he is always polite and never condescending.

But Bella is even more interesting to her than Henry, and that is because she has suddenly become herself. Pat has seen this particularly with women. Bella has suddenly become herself, and yet she has so little energy that she can't quite pull it off. She needs help. Pat wants to help her, but she knows that Bella needs particular help – it will have to come from Henry, there is no one else, but neither Bella nor Henry are conscious of what is entailed. With luck, one of them will stumble on it, and Pat will help them both if she can. These two, mother and son, dance around each other, their arms weaving and twining with the air rather than with each other.

She hears Henry return to the house after Pete Mays leaves. She hears the back screen door slam in that rickety way of screen doors and then pictures him standing in the middle of the kitchen lost in thought and fumbling for the next step. He might telephone that man he works with. He does sometimes. Simon Bowles, who tries to draw her out when he calls and she answers the phone. She can hardly understand him – his English accent is much stronger than Bella's – but she has the satisfaction of knowing that he can hardly understand her either. Scots, he said one time, correctly. "I'm from Wiltshire," he told her, perfectly aware that she had no idea what she meant by that.

But tonight Henry climbs the stairs to the second floor and comes to Bella's door, where he leans in and looks. He sees Pat, knitting, and smiles that soft, full smile of his that's so surprising. "Hi, Pat."

"You go do something you feel like doing," Pat says gruffly. "I'll sit tonight."

And he is gone.

Henry remembers feeling this way when he was little, as though the house is too big for him. He goes to his room, walks to the window, smells the smoke from the forest fires and walks away. He climbs the steps to the attic, looks into the room that used to be his mother's home studio but finds nothing to draw him in. The whole house feels empty tonight, the way the houses of the very old feel when all the things within them begin to imagine themselves ownerless. Aimlessly he opens the only other door on the third floor and reaches for the switch beside it, allowing an inadequate yellow light. It is a windowless, unfinished room full of boxes and a few broken chairs, and very hot.

Vaguely curious, he inspects the nearest boxes. They aren't neatly stacked or organized but have been pushed randomly toward the eaves. He pulls one out by the torn flap of the box closure and sends up a cloud of dust that makes him sneeze. Looking in, he sees cancelled checks and bank statements from years earlier. He inspects two more with similar contents and becomes impatient. Surely there is something more interesting.

After half a dozen boxes, one of which contains some old toys and his first ballet slippers, a surprising find which throws him a little off-balance, he encounters a more orderly and promising stash, two boxes that are neatly closed and labeled in black marker: England. These he carries into the upstairs studio where it is a little cooler. He sits down on the floor and opens the first one.

There are business papers in these as well, but also a small bundle of letters held together with rubber bands which have rotted and which fall apart when he pulls on them. He extracts a page from the top envelope and reads the small, neat handwriting quickly before looking at the signature at the bottom: Adrian. His uncle. All of the letters are from the period between Bella's arrival in Deep River in 1946, and shortly after Max's death in 1954. The first few are cursory accounts of family affairs: their parents' various illnesses; the state of the family property and Adrian's own frustration in having to deal with everything; his congratulations on Henry's birth. The contents become more interesting after 1949, with vague references to some unhappiness Bella is experiencing.

11 February, 1950.

Dearest Bella,

Recv'd your letter with picture of Henry and must concede he's slightly better-looking than the average enfant. It's good that you now have him to give your love to – the older I get the more I think that children, at least when they are new, are far better than lovers any day to have in one's life. I'm sure you will remember my oblique attempts to say something about Max – oblique because we were brought up not to speak ill of guests. I am sure he means well but can't get past his own muck. No, he never spoke to me about his experiences in Belgium, but they were sure to have been horrible – everybody's were. You were always a forgiving soul, but in forgiving his behavior on the basis of his war experiences or anything else don't let yourself become his doormat. You were never good at confrontation – as I recall, you found other ways to stand your ground!

20th April, 1951.

Dearest Bella,

There is no sense in your coming if it is too difficult on your end. I know you don't want to leave Henry, and if Max refuses to let you bring him, well...there isn't much you can do. You can't get here in time for Father's funeral anyway, and Mother is unlikely to recognize you. It is only for my own sake – and yours, dear Bella, that I regret the difficulties.

There are things here you will want, and I will send them when I can. Unless you think otherwise, I plan to put the house up for sale and move Mother in with me, with a nurse. I have plenty of room and to be honest I don't think it likely to be for more than a year or so. I'll survive! There isn't much money, as I think you know, and most of the money from the house will have to go toward paying Father's debts and for Mother's care.

27ᵗʰ July, 1951

Dearest Bella,

I seem to recall that today is the day that Henry embarks upon the "terrible two's," I believe they call it (who are "they?"). Please give him my hearty felicitations, although by the time you receive this they will be a month past due I'm sure. Perhaps he won't notice.

I have just sent off to you, via boat, six boxes: four containing china, carefully wrapped, and two of books – the ones you mentioned and some others that I recall you liked and were probably embarrassed to ask for in fear of appearing greedy. But you are the reader in the family, remember, and perhaps your son will take after you? So if you want you can think of my half as a birthday gift. I like the idea of books but not the books themselves, alas; and I promise you, I won't be having any children to pass things on to. I won't list the pieces of china, too boring. These are the books: Box 1: Aeschylus; Apuleius (2); Beowulf; Blake; Cervantes; Chaucer; Chretien de Troyes; Coleridge (3); Dante (3); Donne; Dostoyevsky; Forster (4); Goethe (4); Hardy (2); both Lawrences (DH, 4; TH:SP); Mabinogian (Lady G); Malory (2); Omar Khayyam; Petrarch, Rabelais. Box 2: Loeb Classical Library, full set (Homer, etc.);Oxford Bk of Eng. V.; Shakespeare (40 v.); Virgil; Bach keyboard (3); lute songs (Dowland, etc.) – sorry can't send lute but thought you might enjoy the nostalgia! I'm sure you have a piano…

Will send more if can.

Love,

A.

He reads this letter twice, three times, his body so overtaken by weakness that he crawls toward the side of the room and leans his head against the wall panting for air. The letter is still in his hand. He reads it again - reads slowly and carefully the list of books as though he has never seen the names before, as though they didn't materially exist on the shelves downstairs, each one possessively inscribed with the large flowing signature of his father. His mind is working so slowly that it can't understand what he is reading. At first he wonders why Adrian would have his father's books, and why send them to Bella instead of to Max. Little by little he fits together the only and obvious explanation, and then must ask a different *why*, one much more difficult to comprehend.

The letter falls onto the floor, and his eye settles on the other box, the one he hasn't opened. Does it harbor another secret, companion to the one he has discovered? He cannot bring himself to look. If Bella were well, he would rush downstairs right now, push Pat out of the room, close the door and confront her. But she is not well, she is dying, which makes the confrontation that much more imperative.

After awhile he returns to the box and kneels over it staring into its depths. He is thirty, and for nearly thirty years these letters have sat up here waiting for him. For nearly thirty years, his mother has led him to believe she is someone she is not. Or that his father was someone he was not. What did that first letter say? He finds it and reads, "...as I recall, you found other ways to stand your ground!"

He had better muster his courage and go downstairs.

But instead he falls asleep, leaning against the wall beneath the gable window. When he awakens the ugly light hurts his eyes and his sinuses are clogged with the attic grime. It is nearly dawn; the sky is a hazy monochrome with hints of orange outlining the hilltops, and the air still smells of smoke. He tiptoes downstairs carrying the letters and looks into his mother's room. Bella and Pat are both asleep. He puts the letters on the bed in his room, showers, shaves and puts on a clean tea shirt and jeans. He would like to work out but is afraid that the floorboards will creak and disturb the two women. He goes out the front door and stands on the porch. Mist lies low in the valley, partly a result of the fires. He walks down the hill to the flat place above where they keep the car and works out there, something he hasn't done before. If the air had been fresher, he thinks it might be wonderful, dancing out here in the dawn light. As it is, his old dream comes starkly to life, of him trapped in the place he has taken such pains to escape – trapped, almost, of his own accord, yet dancing, an endless, useless, unobserved round. He stops dancing, kicks at the sod with his sneaker toe, shivers with fatigue, and goes back indoors.

Pat is in the kitchen making coffee.

"How did Bella sleep?" he asks, accepting the silently proffered cup and perching on the edge of the table.

"Pretty well. She got up once and was awake for an hour or so. She likes to talk sometimes, in the middle of the night."

"Not very restful for you, though."

'I don't mind." Pat doesn't ask questions, but Henry senses a question.

"What?"

"You stayed in the attic all night."

"I fell asleep up there. Pat, did you know my father?"

"Well, no, not really. My husband worked under him though, the last year or so before your daddy died. Thought highly of him – said he'd do anything to help the men under him - go to bat with the higher ups and so forth."

"What did you and Bella talk about last night?"

"Oh, the past as usual. This and that. She says she hasn't seen you dance since you left home."

"No, she hasn't."

"Hmmm." While they are talking, Pat has prepared a tray for Bella, which she picks up and holds out toward Henry. "Want to take this up?"

Sometimes he feels as though Pat knows everything that's going on. "Sure," he says.

Bella is awake and looks pleased that he is the one who has brought her breakfast. He sets it on the bedside table and helps her to sit up, plumping the pillows and getting her situated. She looks a little better this morning.

He has retrieved the letters from his room. He sits in the rocking chair while she sips her tea, playing with the envelopes where he has shoved them into the pocket of his jeans. After she has eaten a little toast, he rises and sits on the edge of her bed, pulling the letters out as he does so. His chest feels light and fluttery.

"Bella." She is surprised by something in his voice and frowns a little. "I went up into the attic last night and snooped."

She laughs. "Well, that's the only thing attics are good for, I always thought. Not much up there as I recall."

"I found letters," –he holds them out- "from your brother. I read them." He continues to hold them out to her, but she doesn't take them.

"You can put them down," she says after awhile. "I don't want to reread them right now."

Slowly Henry's hand drops until it lies on the coverlet with the letters under it. "You've misled me all my life," he says gently. "I don't understand. They are your books, all the books I devoured, treasuring the thought that Max would be so proud of me, because I liked the things he liked. Do you know, after he died I used to sit on the floor by the bookcase with one of the books open on my lap so I could run my fingers over his signature with my eyes closed, pretending it was his face, and yet I have no memory at all of that kind of affection between us. It should have been your signature. Why did he do that? It was defacement. Why did you let him?"

Bella sets her teacup on the tray and crosses her arms. There is a hint of her old flamboyance and Henry feels an involuntary flash of annoyance, but she grows serious. "Now that he's fallen off your pedestal you intend to grind your heel into him? It must be one extreme or the other?"

"Then explain to me, so I can understand. From the beginning."

"From the beginning. How do I do that? Well, I'll try. We met because my brother brought him home one weekend. Adrian and Max met through some sort of effort to welcome the Americans to the war. They never became good friends, and I only saw Max that one time before he went to the front. The war in Europe was over when I saw him next, and I thought that he had changed, but who wouldn't have? So it was a very quick courtship and we married for the wrong reasons: I, to prove yet again to my family that I was an independent spirit; he, in order that my Anglo semi-aristocratic antecedents would become his. Oh yes, he longed for that, but if anyone had told me at the time I would have laughed at them. I found out later.

"Your father...your father was a troubled man, Henry. Whether he had been before the war of course I have no way of knowing. Probably he was – it went too deep to be recent. He was very much respected at work, because he would have done anything for the men under him – I presume that was true in the war too. But at home – well, he found out very quickly that he didn't like me. The more I tried to please him, the more annoyed he was. You've seen how I become, and don't deny it." Henry smiled and looked down at his hands.

"To be fair to myself, I don't think it was entirely me. He shunned intimacy, but he loved sex. I don't think he liked women very much, but he was dependent upon them. He wasn't faithful, and he could be ruthless if he wanted something, or if he expected you to stay out of his way. You would have thought that I would come to hate him, but it didn't happen. The worse he was, the harder I tried. The harder I tried, the more he abused me. No, he never hit me – that might have been easier, but he was more subtle than that. Over time, he simply destroyed what little self-respect I had. He could reduce me to a sodden heap at his feet. The books – the books were part of that English aristocratic façade that he craved, so one time when he was tongue-lashing me over yet another of my failings, I gave him the books. I wasn't reading them anymore anyway, and if I had been, they were still in the house – what difference did it make? He wrote his name in all of them that same night. He wanted me to remember that they weren't mine anymore.

"In short, he wanted nothing to be mine anymore, except what little of himself he allowed me, and I went along with it. But when I inherited the pittance from my family, I decided to open the school – *that*, I thought

215

would be mine, and he managed to hijack that too – I didn't have enough money to do the whole thing, so he handled it, borrowed the rest of the money. He did it in such a way that nothing was actually mine – it was either his, or in trust to you, with a provision that I be looked after, as though I were the child, not you. Of course, it was my own fault for trusting him, but in those days, and in my family, that's what women did.

"But when you showed an interest in dancing, and not only an interest but a gift, I saw at last what he could not appropriate. When I told him about your talent, he laughed at me. He said that "no son of his was going to be a ballet dancer." He said you'd lose interest, and even before he died, I knew he was wrong, and that I was going to do everything I could to assure that he was wrong.

"And then he died, and it was so propitious in a way that I felt as though I had willed it. I did what I swore I would – gave you the best training I was capable of giving – but the guilt I felt was huge and I assuaged it by convincing myself that a boy needed his father, needed to believe in his father, more than in his mother. So I helped you build your shrine of books and worship at it, played down my teaching and played up the fact that he had funded the school, told you what a loving man and father he had been. I wanted you to believe that he was good. I wanted you to model yourself on a good man. "

Thankfully, Bella answers Henry's question without

his needing to ask it. "He was shot by a man whose wife he was having an affair with," she says. "Such a sordid, petty ending, although Roy did a little hurried rearranging of the crime scene, and the police decided it had to do with some bad blood at work. I didn't want you to know, but I don't have the strength anymore not to answer your questions." She is crying now, not making a sound, but the tears flood her eyes and spill over, a cataract down her face and nightgown. Henry climbs over her and propping the spare pillow behind him sits next to her with his arm around her.

"It's all right. Don't cry. It's better that I know – I'm glad I know."

She puts her head against his shoulder so that the tears wet his shirt thoroughly. "All those years you never came home – my greatest fear was that you had become like him, that having the model of him in your mind wasn't enough, and that you had inherited that quality he had – of self-centeredness – that allowed him to be so ruthless."

"Perhaps I did inherit it," Henry says musingly. "I am self-entered, and I can be ruthless. Sometimes I think that I have no feeling at all for other people."

"No." She is very emphatic. "You think that sometimes, because of what you must do for your work. But Max would never have done for me what you have done these past two months."

217

"I owe you everything," Henry tells her wonderingly, taking her hand and stroking it. "Everything."

"No more than I owe you."

A few minutes later, Henry speaks again. "In spite of everything you didn't stop loving him."

"No. He wasn't a good man, but he wasn't a bad man either. Although it probably wouldn't have made any difference if he had been."

8. THE ACTIVIST

A few days later, Pete brings Roy to see Bella. It is late afternoon, after Pete's school day has ended. Bella has come downstairs for the occasion, helped by the exasperating Mary, who feels it's her job to hover. "Oh, stop it, Mary," Bella says, finally. "Go make tea and let me have a little peace." She has dressed, and put on makeup. She doesn't know why she feels particularly strongly about not appearing ill in front of Roy. Pete has called to ask her if they can come. It is short notice, and Henry has gone into Kramer, to the school – she insists that he do so every day just to give him time away from her, and she can see that it does him good. He is working on some new piece, and the two little students are the one lighthearted aspect of his current life. She believes he would want to be here when Roy comes, but she herself is ambivalent about their meeting.

She hears Roy and Pete come up the stairs to the front porch and rises carefully from the sofa where she has placed herself, determined to answer the door before Mary hears them. Carefully, balancing by holding onto the wall or a piece of furniture, she makes her way to the door and opens it. Roy fills the doorway. She has forgotten how big he is, tall and big-boned. The muscle has mostly fallen away now though; his face is lined and his hair and eyebrows nearly white.

He has not forgotten how small she is, but the signs of illness shock him and his immediate thought is of what an effort this meeting must be for her. He has an impulse to embrace her, but she holds out her hand and he takes it, after twenty-five years of total silence.

The last time she saw him was on the day he finished the retaining wall in the back of the house, where Henry still likes to sit. He would perch there sometimes when Roy was working on it and watch, occasionally asking a question while she kept an eye on them from the window beside the kitchen door. For a few weeks after the wall was finished, Henry asked when Roy was coming again but sensing her reluctance he soon stopped.

She steps aside as she motions for Roy to enter, her hand trembling from weakness on the doorknob, but she blocks Pete's way.

"Hello Pete. Do you mind? Roy and I have a lot of catching up to do. Linda Paisley should be home from work soon – you could drop in on her for an hour or so." She has thought this out carefully.

"Where is the girl?" Bella asks when she has settled herself on the living room sofa again and Roy is sitting ramrod straight in the armchair across from her.

A hint of a smile touches Roy's mouth although there is little of humor about his face. "Sarah," he reminds her. "She's thirty-two years old now, Mz. Oliver. Not a girl. I couldn't bring her today." He has no urge to tell Bella why.

"I would like to have seen her," Bella says. "You tried to help me, back after Max died. I never forgot that." She can't help being gruff, or sounding peevish, he thinks. It's the habit of her thought concerning him, and, besides, she is ill. Still, after all these years does she think he will suddenly blubber over her, or that she ought to blubber over him? If so, she has another thing coming. He sits looking at her, waiting for her to say more.

"I didn't know anything about you," she continues, "except that you stuck by Max and he trusted you. You had to know what he was like, that he could be – mean. I was afraid of you – that was the only reason I let you build our wall out back. But when you were here, and I watched you building, saw how you were with Henry, I wasn't afraid of you anymore – I was afraid of what you knew. I wanted to be done with Max myself – I didn't yet quite grasp the impossibility of that - and I didn't want Henry to think anything but the best of his father. I preferred not to have anything to do with you. It wasn't your fault, but I never told you that."

"I knew," Roy says in his soft voice. "So what's changed? You worried about your soul?"

Bella laughs. "Do I even have one? No, I'm not worried about my soul. I guess lying around gives me too much time to think. I began to wonder about what you knew, how you got to be so important to Max. I never had before – particulars were the last things I wanted. And now, keeping silent doesn't matter anymore – to Henry or to me, although perhaps it does to you. Henry knows the truth about Max. He found some letters I had put in the attic."

Roy moves his hands from his knees to the arms of the chair and sits back a little. "Max didn't trust me, exactly," he says after awhile. "He just knew he could say what he liked around me because I was *colored*. It didn't matter what he said, because of that. But he was mixed up about it, like he was about a lot of things. One side of him said I didn't matter and another side said something else. He had a kind of attraction to what you might call the downtrodden and the underdog."

"Why did you put up with it? You protected him, from public opinion, if nothing else. If you'd wanted to, you could have ruined his reputation."

"I didn't see it that way. I agreed with him – I saw myself as *colored* just as much as he did. But it wasn't only that. People thought I idolized Max, but that wasn't exactly true. As I said, he was mixed up. He might have been a bigot but he was also the only man in management who spoke up for the workers." She can see that he is mulling over whether or not to tell her something, so she waits. "And then there was my little sister, Mae. She adored him, and he hung around her like a fly around honey, till she got pregnant. I flattered myself, just like she flattered herself – that we were good enough for him. It gets like that sometimes, when you don't have much. Of course, I learned quickly he was that way with most women. He liked slumming. But Mae didn't know it, and she never found out, thank god. It would have killed her. What am I saying? He managed to kill her anyway, by making her pregnant, and then when Sarah was born – even before she was born - he wanted to walk away. I wouldn't let him. I made a deal with him, that I would raise Sarah but he had to be good to Mae and to pay Sarah's way. He got off easy, because Mae died two days after the baby came. It wasn't blackmail – he knew he was in the wrong, and what could I really do anyway, except threaten? I would never have let Sarah know what she had for a father. I raised her to believe she had fine parents, not a silly girl for a mother and a mean, screwed-up woman-chaser for a father." He stops speaking, astonished that after all the years of silence it has been this easy to say everything, and in so few words.

Bella nods slowly. It is only confirmation of what she has worked out in her own mind. It is why she had wanted Roy to bring Sarah, so that she could look at the girl. It was after Pete's comment that he thought he must have met her before that she began to piece things together.

"And Sarah herself?" she asks Roy. He looks puzzled. "Did it benefit her greatly, not to know who or what he was?"

He shakes his head. "I think you know it didn't."

"You had better tell me about her."

And so he does, in his understated, even manner, never raising his voice or giving any sort of emotional emphasis to what he has to tell. He describes her childhood, her hyperactivity, her waywardness, and her elfin early charm. He makes no excuses for his own indulgence of her or his failure to recognize her problems with learning and socialization, or his unwillingness to accept that despite all his efforts she possesses both a hardness and a neediness uncomfortably reminiscent of Max. Dispassionately, he describes her disappearance and absence, his ten-year search and finding her in Staunton, aged beyond her years and drug addicted. Finally, he tells about the events of a few nights earlier, when he, with Linda and Pete, had taken her to the emergency room for the cuts she had inflicted on herself, only to be told by the doctor that he couldn't release her because she is a danger to herself and others, and that she would be sent to the state facility to be evaluated and probably institutionalized indefinitely. Only then does he reveal, just a little, the raw state of his emotions.

"That place has an awful reputation – no one lets their kin go there if they can help it. I might as well have left her to her heroin over there in Staunton."

"No," Bella says. "We can do something about that." She reaches for the telephone, dials Doc Roberts' office number, and gets his receptionist. "Is James still there? I want you to get a message to him – please have him call as soon as he can. No, I'm fine, but it's important. Good." She hangs up. "This is something I can help you with, or Henry can. We'll find some place for her to go, don't worry." She finds, lately, that it is difficult to keep the tears from flowing. She blinks her eyes quickly and takes a deep breath. "All this saintliness we've tried to cultivate in Max's name! What an absurd concept. It's kept all of us apart, all these years – Henry and me, you and me, perhaps you and Sarah. Well, it's over now. It was worst for you, with no resources and Sarah not even your own child – there was nothing tangible to deal with. At least I had dancing to give to Henry – it's the only thing that saved us. Now, would you mind going to the kitchen and seeing what Mary's done with the tea? I think I must have frightened her away."

Henry arrives home to find Pete sitting on the top step leading to the front porch. "Hello. What are you doing here?"

"I brought Roy up to see your mother. I have to

wait to take him home, but I'm afraid to interrupt them. I guess they're reconciling – remember what I mentioned to you awhile back – what Roy said to me?"

Henry sits down beside Pete. "Yes, I remember. And what else have you been up to?" he asks.

Pete shrugs. "School's started, so I'm busy with that. I went flying on the weekend with my friend John Daley and took pictures of the fires, the terrain – a whole new world for me, up there. I wasn't so keen on flying, but I think I could get used to it – it's worth it for the pictures."

"Seeing Linda?"

"A little," Pete says reluctantly.

"Well, I miss you stopping by the studio."

"What have you been doing?"

"I have a new commission, for an English company. And my two little students have multiplied into four – they each brought a friend; they're a nice diversion from too much seriousness."

"So you're doing that."

"Sure – I promised their mother I would. We're working on a little piece."

"And Bella?"

"Bella's up and down. Her spirits are remarkably up; her body generally down."

"It's because of you – her spirits."

Henry doesn't deny it. "It's been good for us, this time together. Too bad it's taken terminal illness to let us finally get to know one another."

"You'll leave, when – this is over."

"Yes. All the muck in my brain when I first came seems really distant and inconsequential now. You know…" He hesitates. "A couple of weeks ago I thought of asking you if you'd want to come to New York with me."

Pete regards him with astonishment and then laughs. "Right. I can just see that, not to mention all the purely practical issues. You don't need to try to make me feel better, Henry. I understand. Besides, I have my own ambivalence, as you well know."

Henry nods. "I'm not trying to make you feel better. At least, I don't think I am. I think what I'm trying to do is to open myself up a little more."

"That's a good thing to do," Pete agrees, "but I don't think it is going to change who and what you are first and foremost: an artist." He says the words in a perfectly normal tone of voice, but beneath them, his own battle still rages.

"Let's go in," Henry says. "See what they're up to."

They are drinking tea.

Bella looks up when they enter, and Roy sets down his cup and stands. "Well, Roy, I'm sure you can tell who this is," Bella says, and the two men shake hands as if they are strangers meeting for the first time. Watching them, Bella – a woman who believes regret to be a waste of time - is filled with her only true moment of regret. She can picture them so clearly twenty-five years earlier, talking while Roy builds the wall, completely at ease in one another's company.

The awkwardness of the three men with each other bores her, but Bella isn't sure if it is wise to put an end to the polite tea-sipping and surface chat that occupy the minutes which follow. She is relieved when Pete decides that it is time for Roy and him to go. When Henry returns from seeing them out and begins to pick up the dirty cups to take to the kitchen, she stops him.

"Put them down, Henry. There is something I need to talk to you about." He does as he is told, carefully replacing the delicate cup and saucer that had looked so wonderfully incongruous in Roy's hand right where he had left it and sitting in his father's chair.

And so from Bella he learns more truths about his father and that he has a half-sister. He watches his mother as she speaks. It is late afternoon, and the last ray of light is coming through the window and lighting the back of her head, giving her a sort of halo or aura. She had neatened up, he notices for the first time, for Roy's visit. The light is beautiful, and her voice is beautiful, something he has never noticed or thought in his life before. She speaks softly, and her voice is neither high nor low. There are no tricks now; she is not playing for attention, or acting ridiculous because she doesn't know how she is supposed to act. She is not speaking in order to annoy. She has draped her arm across the back of the sofa, and now he sees how long her fingers are – like dancers' legs. Intrigued, he looks down at his own elegant hands. He isn't really hearing the meaning of her words; the beauty of her voice, and the light, and her hand on the sofa back are all that matter…

"I didn't explain this to you the other night, Henry – I didn't think I would need to, since you'll find it all out soon enough. I have no control over my property – technically, it isn't mine at all. It's yours, but pays me a sort of allowance. Another of Max's ploys, to insure my school didn't plunge us into ruination I suppose. He didn't believe women capable of handling finances – quite a Victorian, really, your father. I want you to use your control over the estate to help Roy now, and find Sarah a good hospital; we owe them that, and I don't think you mind – do you? You will have to go to the accountant and work things out, sign things. You aren't listening." He jerks his eyes away from her hand, and smiles.

"Not really. Can you say it over again? You want me to help Roy?"

She explains it all again, and he listens this time, nodding. "I've put in a call to James – he'll know what to do about a hospital. But you'll have to do the rest – actually arrange it, and pay for it. My allowance isn't enough, so it will have to come out of your principle. Do you mind very much? There probably won't be a lot left over for you. The good hospitals are expensive. I just don't see how we can not...."

He comes to sit beside her and lifting the beautiful hand kisses it and holds it to his face, so she will understand and not fret. "I don't mind at all, Bella. You are right about everything, and I don't need money - I have plenty. As long as you are taken care of, we can give all the rest to them. Don't worry. I'll see that it's all done, and that they're never in need." He feels her hand relax, and knows that exhaustion is overtaking her. "We need to get you back to bed now." He offers to carry her, but she insists on walking, so he puts his arm around her waist and supports her slowly up the stairs. "You are a sort of fairy godmother," he comments as he helps her get ready for bed. "I don't think I would have thought of doing that for them."

"You would have if you'd known the situation, but you didn't – Roy and I both kept it from you. Will you apologize to Mary for me before she leaves? I upset her earlier – didn't you notice how unusually quiet the house is? But I don't think I'm quite up to seeing her again tonight."

But Mary has already left without saying goodbye, so the apology will have to wait. He clears away the teacups and washes them. Pat doesn't come tonight - it is his turn to sit up with Bella. He wishes, a little, that Pat it wasn't. He likes Pat's quiet company, and tonight he is both tired and preoccupied and wouldn't mind lying on his own bed. His day in the studio had been particularly productive and exciting, and then the children had come for an hour and he had put them through some of his new steps, which had made them all laugh. How strange then to return to the house and learn that he has a sister – a sister whom he must support. And even stranger, this feeling of calm that attends the knowledge. It is not happy or welcome knowledge, of a new family member. It is too late in life to gain a sister anyway, but Bella has been very careful to explain the hopelessness of Sarah's situation and to let him know, without actually saying it, that there is need for detachment. He doesn't think he will find that difficult. So, even though this new knowledge is unwelcome, there is an inevitability about it that makes the fact of its arrival a relief.

On the nights that Pat doesn't come his practice is to read or think or make notes in the living room, and then go up to Bella around eleven. It is after that when she is likely to be restless or to need someone. She scoffs at the notion that someone must sit up with her all night, but Henry finds it more restful to sit in the chair than to be in his own room with the door open, constantly fighting sleep and straining to listen for her. She encourages him to leave the light on and read, but he rarely does. The dim glow of the nightlight casts a mood that draws him in and lets him dream dreams of his own choosing. Tonight, however, his mind needs as complete a respite as possible from his immediate environment. Before he goes to Bella he calls Simon Bowles, finds him at home, and for a precious hour discusses musical ideas and dance steps, and listens to dance world gossip.

"What did she want?" Pete asks as he and Roy drive home.

Roy looks out the window. "She wanted to apologize," he says, "for taking against me all those years ago. "

"Why did she?" Pete asks. "Did she ever say?"

"We both already knew why," Roy says enigmatically. "She didn't have to say."

Pete frowns in puzzlement but doesn't say anything.

Roy has weighed in his mind what he ought to tell Pete and still isn't sure, but he decides that if Pete can't figure out for himself why Sarah looks familiar, then he's not going to tell him. Roy knows it's the residue of racism. If you take away Sarah's honey skin and brown eyes and frizzy hair, and replace all the signs of drug use and poverty with those of healthy physical exercise and love of what you do in life, then Sarah might well *be* Henry. Any fool could see it. As for the rest of what they talked about, it needs to settle. There will be plenty of time to explain how Sarah comes to be in a private hospital, if it really happens.

But Roy doesn't want to be rude. "You never said how you liked flying in an airplane, Pete."

"Linda says with John Daley at the controls it's taking your life in your hands, but I was so preoccupied with taking pictures, I forgot to pay attention. Pretty amazing. I'll bring some down to show you once I've developed them. I'm going up again this coming weekend." He smiles at Roy. "Wanna come?"

Roy laughs, a throaty chuckle. "No-thank-you-Sir. You've sure changed your tune. Couldn't pay me enough to do something like that." At least it's a change of subject.

9. THE DANCE

"I made some spaghetti," Pat volunteers as Henry washes his hands at the kitchen sink. She is becoming positively talkative.

They eat together at the kitchen table. The spaghetti sauce is excellent. "You have Italian blood, Pat," he tells her as he spoons more sauce over a second helping of pasta and sprinkles Parmesan over it.

"That's right. My mother was a Milo. I grew up Catholic – went to the big stone church on the road right before you cross the bridge to Kramer. I'm not Catholic now though."

Henry raises his eyebrows. "Excommunicated?"

"Too much catechism is more like it. I was born skeptical, just like Grandpa Milo – but he was afraid of Grandma." She chews a bite and swallows it then ventures a question. "What are you doing, down there in the dance school?" They never talk about Henry's work, or about Henry.

He looks up, a little surprised, and sees the genuine interest in her face. "You want the short sketchy explanation or the details?"

"The details would be interesting," she replies.

"Well, when I get there, I put on some music – something like Mozart, or Bach – then I warm up, get my juices flowing, for about an hour. Stretches first, then gradually work into movement more specifically dance related. After that, I practice – work on particular pieces – old ones sometimes, or on the one I'm making up now, for a dance company in England."

"For Mr. Bowles?"

"Yes. I forgot you've talked to him." His eyelids flicker – she has noticed, one of his ways for pushing aside emotion - just before he continues. "Assuming I can, I'll go to London at the first of the year and start rehearsing them."

"You mean – if you're not needed here anymore."

He looks straight at her. "Yes."

"I don't think you will be, Henry," she says quietly.

"You've done this a lot of times, haven't you?"

Pat nods. "Almost more than I can count."

"Don't you get worn out with it – so much death?"

She watches him, the long hands lightly clenched on either side of the plate, the bent head of shiny straight hair that suddenly pulls up to reveal his surprising face. "No, I don't," she tells him. "Every single time, I'm amazed anew, to tell the truth. You start out being disgusted by the helplessness and loss of physical control, but then you stop feeling that way. The person's whole life is condensed, encapsulated, in the last few months and weeks, so that all the physical degradation becomes nothing compared to the richness that is revealed. It's as though they've become a wonderful storybook, there for you to read, if you're interested. Haven't you noticed that yourself?"

"Yes, I think I have."

Henry insists on washing the dishes. Pat drinks coffee and smokes her one cigarette of the day. "You're mother's mentioned several times how she's not seen you dance since you were a boy."

"That's becoming a refrain with you, Pat."

"Well, I think it's a pity."

"It's too late now."

"Why too late? You're here – she's here, for a little longer. I think you should do something about it."

Henry turns off the water and, facing her, leans against the sink. "Where?"

"If it's done right, she could be brought to the dance school. That would be the best place, wouldn't it?"

"Yes."

"I'll call Doc Roberts. I bet he'd help. Would you mind if he was there, and if I was?" Henry's face is more animated than she has ever seen it. If his dancing is like that, then it must be something.

"Okay. Yes," he says, his mind already flown from her. He pushes away from the sink. "Can you call him tonight? We should do it as soon as possible, maybe Saturday or Sunday. I'm going to go back to the studio tonight." He heads for the stairs, to look in on Bella and get his wallet and the car keys. He turns around in the doorway and smiles at Pat, one of his rare, disarming smiles. "Thank you Pat – you're something else."

She rolls her eyes as he disappears into the hall, but inside she feels warm and happy. Really, she thinks, here I am fifty and sensible, and there he is thirty and queer, otherwise I could almost convince myself I've lost my heart to him.

He rarely comes to the studio at night although it is only a fifteen-minute drive into Kramer. He finds it depressing, driving up into the empty potholed lot, seeing the lights on the coal tipple across the river, smelling, too often, the odor of rotten egg released by the chemical plant ten miles down river. Tonight when he steps out of the car, he can see the glows of four fires up in the mountains. It hasn't rained in six weeks now, not a drop, and the temperatures are still in the eighties during the day, falling only a little at night.

He has told Simon that the new work will be to Bach, *The Well-Tempered Clavier*, and that he wants to do all of Book I: 12 dances, one for each set of Prelude and Fugue. Simon had laughed.

"I'm dead serious," Henry said.

"That's two hours of dance. No, Henry."

"An hour and fifty-seven minutes, actually, without intermission."

"The Bach is fine – it will contrast well with the other work I'm using next season - but you'll have to pick the preludes and fugues. Half-hour at most." That meant he could get away with forty minutes – more than a third of the work.

"If you say so. But I'm going to set them all, eventually, and one day they will all be danced together – wait and see."

"It'll be like one of those cello suite marathons."

"More or less. Will you start looking for a pianist? I want the piano on the stage."

"Do you have a short list for pianists?"

" I'll send it to you."

He switches on the light and goes straight to the record player, turning it on and setting the needle on the record already on the turntable, Gould's recording of the *Well-Tempered Clavier*. Henry still hasn't decided which sections to use, whether to piece several together to make a coherent dance, or simply start at the beginning and use the first few. That would work well, if Simon will allow a forty-three minute piece, finishing with E-major.

But even without that decision he has made good beginnings on some of the dances, and he wants to show them to Bella. He wants to know what she thinks, whether she will notice that he has turned the preludes into fugues. Pat's suggestion that he perform them for her, amounting almost to insistence, makes him feel like a small child again, who can make everything all right by dancing. Suddenly he imagines the discussions he has never had with Bella, about style and technique, about music, and practice, and imagination. He doesn't even know what she likes, or what she used to like. Never before has he thought to ask her, and now it is too difficult. Since the night he found the letters, he has felt close to her – and, he knows, she to him – but they share a lifetime of restraint and secretiveness. They are both masters of those skills; renouncing them is not so easy.

But this, he can do: show Bella his new dances, and she will know instinctively what he wants from her – not approval, unless it is earned, but good honest criticism. She always gave him that, never coddled him as a student – her teaching is the basis of everything he's done. He has been teaching the children one of the preludes, with simple steps they might eventually be able to handle. For now, they are terrible, but he will have them show Bella what they can do, and it will remind her of her own teaching days and perhaps make her happy.

It is Thursday night; the children come on Friday afternoon, and he can rehearse them, then they could perform for Bella on Saturday or Sunday afternoon. The children's mother might come, and Doc Roberts, and Pat, if they must. He doesn't want anyone else.

Pete is driving home from the airport late and passes Bella's old dance studio, where he sees lights in the window. He is tired and exhilarated both, having met John Daley right after school to go flying. It is becoming an obsession, this taking pictures from the air, an antidote to human interaction, which always trips him up. Always trips everyone up, he admits when he's being honest, but that doesn't mean he has to stand for it. The fear of flying, which had once paralyzed him, has been replaced by an almost manic and constant wish to be up in the air, seeing all the familiar specifics turn into one great aesthetic generality. Sometimes John flies low over the forests and – when the wind was favorable, blowing the smoke in a single direction – over the fires. Then, Pete feels like Gulliver and almost imagines he could reach down and uproot a tree between two fingers or douse the fires with a little well-aimed spit. But there is the other side too, that he might come crashing down, not fatally, but landing among those miniature trees and breaking them, or in the river, splashing all the water out, too big and bumbling for this world. But for photographs, it is perfect.

Without even thinking, he turns off the road into the parking lot, cuts the engine and gets out without slamming the door. He can hear the strains of Bach – he knows it's Bach thanks to Henry – the volume is turned up high. Once he is out of the car, he hesitates for a moment, but after a day of teaching, an afternoon and evening of flying and picture-taking, no dinner and two beers with John Daley, he is not in a self-conscious state. The blind is drawn down to cover most of the window, but he can see that Henry is working something out, experimenting with a series of movements over and over again. He tries the door, finds it unlocked, and opens it.

Henry's back is to him so that when he raises his head and sees in the mirror that someone is standing near the door where it is too shadowy to identify who it is, he is startled and jumps, turning reflexively as though he must defend himself. Pete moves out of the shadows.

"Pete!"

"I didn't mean to startle you. I was driving by and

241

saw the lights." Henry walks forward, Bach blaring behind him, and Pete meets him in the middle of the floor. It is like flying, somehow, like being Gulliver, there is such a careful design to it, almost inhuman. The music adds to the effect of course. It is impossible to talk over it. Pete doesn't even wonder what Henry is thinking. He just says, "I've missed you."

Henry isn't thinking. Pete's sudden appearance has wrenched him from the place where he wants to be, so deep in music and movement that now, forced to stop and consider another person, he feels as though he is slogging through soup. It isn't pleasant. He doesn't hear what Pete says, although he notices his lips moving- it is the first thing that brings him back to thought. What he thinks is that he must *do* something, so he does: he turns the record player off.

"What did you say?"

But now Pete's own self-consciousness has kicked in. He shouldn't have come. "I've disturbed you," he says this time. "I shouldn't be here."

The spell has broken. Henry feels all the energy leave his body. "No, it's all right. I should go home soon anyway. Where were you?" Pete's shyness annoys him tonight. It is probably just the break in his concentration, not the suspicion he has that Pete is playing with him and doesn't even know it. He heads toward the back, where the bathroom is, pees, and shouts, "Do you want a glass of water?"

"Okay."

Pete follows him toward the back of the room. Henry gives him one of the glasses he is holding and sinks down onto the old sofa. Tentatively, Pete perches himself at the other end and takes a sip of water. It tastes of chlorine.

"Where have you been?" Henry asks again.

"Taking pictures from an airplane." Pete's awkwardness dissipates as he warms to his description of the flight. He sets the glass down on the floor, and unconsciously slips off his shoes as he uses his hands to describe the feeling of flying and the look of the photographs.

"I'd like to see them," Henry says.

"Would you, truly? You're partly responsible, you know. The pictures I took of you broke new ground for me – opened something up I didn't know was there. I haven't showed you those, either, because – because they are so intimate, I've been afraid to show you."

Henry sits up and folds his legs under himself like a yogi, so that one foot is almost touching Pete's knee. He reaches out and takes Pete's gesticulating hand, strokes it. "Afraid to show me, or afraid to look at them with me?" Henry asks, locking his eyes on Pete's face and making it

243

impossible for Pete to look away.

"Both, probably."

"I was there when you took those pictures, remember? I'd like to see them, but I don't *need* to see them to have a pretty good idea of what they are. They aren't just art – they record something you want to pretend never happened." He strokes Pete's hand, strokes it, and then kisses it; the gentle action is curiously at odds with the raw insistence of his voice. He puts his hands on the back of Pete's neck, those ballet dancer hands, and Pete feels the fingers dance there, lightly at first, hypnotically, and then more emphatically as Henry pulls his head forward so that their lips meet, and it is Pete, not Henry, who is suddenly no more than a living hunger. Henry reaches for Pete's hip, caresses it and scoots him so that they can lie down together on the sofa the way they used to. They are both so tired, so completely exhausted, that physical sensation is the only thing left. Too tired to sleep, too tired to think. It is such a relief to have something else to do.

Much later, Pete responds to Henry's words. "I don't want to pretend it never happened," he says. His mouth is right by Henry's ear, and Henry pulls away so that he can see the expression on Pete's face. He has forgotten what they were talking about. He traces the outer rim of Pete's ear.

"This?" he asks.

"I don't want to pretend, or forget, either one. One day, I hope to find you and me sculpted in our own little memorial niche, to which I can fondly return. Neatly compartmentalized. The alternative, for me, is to have it be something awful."

"Like sin?"

"I suppose so. I grew up Baptist, after all. I'm not like you, Henry. Actually, I'm not sure I even know what you're like – only that we're different. This doesn't matter to you one way or the other, does it? When you return to your old life, you'll just forget."

"This?" Henry asks again. "What exactly *is* "this"? Sex with another man? Friendship? Be specific." But then he doesn't give Pete time to answer; he is off on a trail all his own. "I won't forget. Everything matters to me. I just try not to let myself be emotionally overwhelmed. It's so – sloppy. Incapacitating."

"How do you know? I bet you've never even tried it."

Henry doesn't answer, but he feels, at some dark level, a creepy stirring, the serpent at the bottom of his mind, and knows that he has tried it whether he remembers it or not. The revelation isn't something he's willing to share. "I'm not going to change," he says finally. "I don't want to change. Do you want me to profess love for you? It wouldn't be honest. The only

245

person I would profess love to is Bella – and I wouldn't have been capable of that six weeks ago. Is that brutal? If so, I'm sorry. But I *am* very fond of you. *That* is honest."

"We both compartmentalize, but for different reasons."

"Not so different, I suspect. We do it in order to function. You see me as cold, and I see you as someone in denial." Henry sits up and pulls on his t-shirt, then reaches down and turns on the record player. Bach, turned down lower than before, wafts through the atmosphere of the room like a vapor, changing it. Henry stretches his legs out in front of him, points his toes then flexes his feet, turning his legs in and out from the hip as he rubs his knees. "I enjoy it when you come here. We used to never talk about emotions or attachments, and that was part of what I liked –of what we both liked, I think. But when Linda told me she hadn't been seeing much of you in spite of having been proposed to by you, it seemed to me there might be a problem. I felt sorry for her, but I was worried that you weren't too clear on what was going on." He stopped flexing his legs and turned toward Pete, leaning on one hand. "I wish you would keep coming to see me; I've missed you lately, and when I leave here to return to New York I will miss you – I think I tried to tell you that when I suggested I'd had a fleeting idea of your coming with me. I know it isn't feasible – for either of us – for many reasons. I don't want our friendship to be the source of regret."

"It sounds so simple when you say it. You know who you are…"

"You mean homosexual?" Henry asks sharply. Pete nods. "No I don't know that – not in the definitive sense I think you mean. A friend once told me I was the most out gay person he knew, and then accused me of selfishness because I wasn't actively promoting gay rights. The truth is, I don't think of myself as gay, or straight, or anything in between. If anything is my identity it's my work, not my sexual orientation. Sex with men is less complicated, easier to come by. I enjoy it. At work, I find men and women equally beautiful, desirable, enticing. They are the language of my trade. I don't care whether I'm gay or straight – that's what Ray thought was so "out" about me. Why do you care? Can't you love me, and love Linda too, in whatever way you do, without it becoming some sort of moral statement? Why do you have to define yourself in that way? It seems so demeaning."

"Because everyone defines themselves in that way, except you."

Henry shakes his head, kisses Pete's cheek, stands up and stretches. "You will never convince me of that. Now, watch." He leans down and turns the volume up, so that Bach once again has authority over the room. Then he picks up the needle and sets it on the C-minor Prelude before walking to the center of the floor.

Pete, on the way home, wonders if he won't be

glad when Henry leaves, except that it means Bella's death, and he doesn't wish for that. Guilt, everywhere, except up in the sky. He would like some peace of mind.

"Doc Roberts says okay," Pat tells Henry on Friday morning. "He'll come and get Bella and me, he says, whichever day you want. You look tired – more tired than usual. I heard you come in but didn't look at the clock."

" It was almost three. Can we decide this evening whether to do it tomorrow or Sunday? I thought it would be fun if my students did a little something – they aren't very good, but Bella might enjoy it. When they come this afternoon, I'll see if there's any hope, and you can let me know how Bella has been today."

"Sounds like a plan."

Henry has to go by the bank on his way to the studio, to discuss setting up an account out of which to pay for Sarah's care. Doc Roberts has finagled her a place in a small private hospital about an hour away, to which she is to be admitted the following week. By the time he has finished with his business at the bank, it is noon. He stops in the diner for a cup of coffee, where people nod to him. As far as Henry knows, they have no idea of who he is, not even his name– but his face has become familiar.

He lets himself into the studio and goes straight to the sofa to sit down. He can hardly imagine working out; he can hardly imagine anything he's so tired. A nice long bath, perhaps. He sips his coffee and looks at the empty sofa cushion beside him, the one Pete was sitting on last night. It was a nice evening, until Pete wanted to spoil it by talking. Was it Pete who wanted to talk? He can't remember now. It might have been himself. In fact, he *does* remember saying something – something that seemed important at the time. It couldn't have been, very, because he doesn't remember it now. He is fond of Pete. He is fond of Pete in a way that makes him sometimes speculate about what it would be like if he were less intense, less committed to work, less talented. He doesn't wish any of those things, but there are moments when he is lonely because of who he is. He knows it's because he's so exhausting to everyone, including himself. He would wear Pete out in no time. He pulls off his sneakers and finds the ratty old ballet slippers under the sofa. He has exactly three hours until the children arrive.

The twins, Mary and Joe, have had more lessons than their two little friends, because they started first. The friends, who only want to come to dance class because Mary and Joe do, are called Lizzie and Frank. Frank is actually the best – he has a budding dancer's physique and something approaching the right attitude. All four are thrilled at the idea of performing, so Henry tells them that they'd better pay attention, and they do. By the end of class, they have arrived at a satisfactory if hugely unpolished program. "Can you be here in the morning, at ten? Tell your parents that I'll provide lunch, then we'll give our performance in the afternoon. You can invite them if you like." The entire project feels refreshingly juvenile to Henry and solemnly adult to the children. The preparation of their little dance prevents him from thinking too closely about his own, which is to follow it: the world premiere of his new, as yet unfinished, work, to the audience that has at last come to mean more to him than any other.

But when he arrives home that evening, Pat gives him bad news.

"Your mother isn't doing well, Henry. She couldn't get out of bed at all today – she won't be able to go to the studio. And on top of that, they say there's a fire started just across the mountain, up above here. " As if the two things went hand in hand. She is standing with a dishtowel in one hand and a bowl in the other. Henry sits down at the end of the table and looks up at her – his eyes have become very black, she notices – how strange that they can do that.

"That's that, then," he says, and his body sags, folds in on itself, making him look suddenly years older, and not like a dancer at all. "I'd better go call my students and tell them it's off." But he doesn't move, except to hold his hands out in front of him and stare at them.

She sets the towel and bowl together on the counter; the bowl hits the counter with a little too much impact and there is a small but distinct cracking sound. "No," Pat says firmly. "No." She walks across and stands right in front of him, her hands on her hips. "Look at me." She puts her finger under his chin and tips it up as though he were a small wayward boy. "You're creative. Think. So you have to do it here. Your mother's room isn't that small – I'll help you move the furniture, and the rugs – it's just one of those thin Persian things, easy to roll up. We'll make it work. The kids can come here – do you really want them to?"

He nods. "I don't know why I want them, but I do. They really are terrible, but they make me happy – maybe they'll make Bella happy too."

"Okay, then. Don't look so forlorn. Go up and see your mother."

He can hear her slightly obstructed breathing from the doorway. She is lying on her back, her face turned away from him. He takes off his shoes and creeps around the foot of her bed to the rocking chair. Her eyes open. "Henry." Her voice is very weak, but her eyes smile at him. "I want you to take that rocking chair back to New York with you," she says. "Even when I'm dead and gone there's going to be some part of me seeing you sitting in it." She tried to laugh. "Isn't it odd, how we imagine such things? My brother used to say that when he died he wanted to be laid in a glass coffin above ground so he could see out. So promise me you'll take the chair, and use it."

Henry smiles and reaches his hand over to touch hers. "I promise."

Later that night Henry calls Simon Bowles. "I've decided to call the Bach dances *Home Letters*," he tells him. "They've begun to attain a certain narrative flow. It's having its world premiere tomorrow. A surprise world premiere – in my mother's bedroom – five unfinished preludes and fugues."

"I wish I could be there."

"I'm glad you can't be," Henry replies.

Henry has arranged to pick up the children himself on Saturday morning, since he must drive to the studio anyway to pick up the record player and records. Either he or Pat will bring them back. Driving to the house, the children shyly well-behaved in the back seat, he notices that the air is thicker than usual with the smell of smoke and remembers Pat saying last night that a new one had started on the back side of their mountain.

In the kitchen, he tells them what they have to do. "You go to the middle of the floor, just like in the studio," he says, "and when the music begins you do what you've practiced. Don't pay any attention to anything else, and don't forget to feel the music. It isn't a very big audience, but it's an important one – she was once a very great dancer herself, and she was my first and most important teacher. You must be quiet going upstairs, and no talking in the hall, so she'll be surprised. Okay?" They nod solemnly, and Henry feels a pricking beneath his eyelids. He turns quickly to speak to Pat, who is in charge of the record player. They have put it in the hallway right outside Bella's door.

"We're ready," Pat says, and grins. "I told her I was taking away the carpet to be cleaned, and that we had to move the furniture to get it out. She's wide awake and sitting up. I told her you'd be up to see her shortly."

The children's piece, a much-simplified version of the first Prelude and Fugue, is less than four minutes long, and they perform it with great care. Bella is delighted. At the end she laughs and claps. "Henry's students. Encore!" she cries. "What a lovely treat. Can't they stay?" she asks as they run out and down the stairs to snacks in the kitchen. Pat sticks her head through the doorway and says as nonchalantly as she can, "just a minute, Mrs. Oliver."

Henry is as nervous as he can ever remember being. Even in this makeshift venue he can't help thinking of the way the light will hit, whether he can clear the furniture without either overreaching or falling short, and without slipping on the bare poplar floor. The room isn't quite big enough for some of the work's spins and jumps, so he has calculated how to make the most of the limited space – he only hopes he has calculated correctly. It is always nerve-wracking the first time he lets someone else see a new work; this one is so unfinished that he would never let anyone but Bella see it, and yet he would almost be less frightened if it were someone else, a formidable New York or Paris or London critic. He feels as though he is about to audition for a place in heaven.

He is standing just behind where Pat is kneeling on the floor beside the record player, her hand on the arm. They hear Bella's tentative voice, "Pat?"

"Just a second, Mrs. Oliver." She looks up at Henry, who takes a deep breath and nods. She sets the needle at the beginning and the strains of the C-major Prelude begin again.

The habits formed through years of discipline in training and performance are just barely enough to govern his passion. He has not expected to be so overtaken by what he, thanks to Bach and his mother, has created. Even as the gentle first movement sweeps him past her bed and into the open floor beyond, he has an overwhelming sense, a mingling of fear and hope, that he won't be able to stop, that the sublime current of sound and motion will turn greedy and pull him into depths he cannot fathom let alone abide. To anchor himself he uses Bella's eyes as his focal point, and they do not fail him.

She doesn't even blink. The steps he has made to elaborate and compete with the brief and lively C-minor Prelude nearly undo him. He overshoots a jump and his knee cracks into the chest of drawers but he doesn't notice any pain, and fitting himself to the space is easier after that. He doesn't think any of the thoughts that were worrying him earlier: that the dances will be incomprehensible as solos, which he doesn't mean them to be; or that he hasn't made the counterpoint – the movement's, not the music's – evident. The music is so profound a force that every time he hears it is the first time, and this is no exception, so that even his raw new work, even he himself, are absorbed into it. Later, when it is over, he will remember and rationalize: the entire magic of art is to find that furthest place beyond which one cannot go and balance there, on the edge of the world.

At the end of the D-major fugue he flies from the corner where he has found himself, across the room to her bed. Bella's cream-colored bed jacket is made of a loose and flowing silky fabric, and when she opens her arms for him the material ripples like wings glanced by sunlight. He bursts into tears. The music has stopped. Pat has closed the door and gone downstairs to praise the children and take them home.

Later in the day, two bouquets of flowers are delivered by the florist in Kramer - one for Henry and one for Bella. They are from Hector Gardner.

The card on Henry's reads: *Sorry to have been so out of touch. Simon gave me your news – congratulations on the world premiere. However long it takes, we'll be here.*

Bella's says: *To the world's greatest teacher and a fine lady, from her admirer, Hector Gardner.*

She has just enough energy left to laugh. "So we've made the *New York Times*. At least I don't have to worry about your future."

10. FLIGHT AND LANDING

On Sunday afternoon Pete goes flying with his friend John Daley, who wants to inspect the fires burning on ridges in the area around Deep River. "Your own neighborhood, Pete," John says jovially and then notices Pete's disturbed expression. "Oh, don't worry. These things have been burning for a month now and only one house has been touched so far. They *look* dramatic, but they aren't. Nothing like the fires out west – I guess the hills shelter them from the wind that might spread them."

"Yes, but if we don't have rain soon, we'll have big trouble," Pete responds. He doesn't feel much like going flying today, or taking more pictures. It seems like a good day to stay in the basement developing the last three rolls.

John makes a nice smooth takeoff, and Pete sits back letting his heartbeat normalize as they follow the river out of town. Thirty miles east they cut north up one of the hollows until thickening smoke below tells them they are approaching the fires. Every now and then they hit a little turbulence and John laughs.

"What's so funny?" Pete demands the first time, bracing himself. The euphoria that he relies upon as a substitute for panic is absent today.

"'A boat on the waves of the heavens,' quotes John. "God, I love flying."

"Where'd you hear that?" Pete asks.

"Hell if I know." John looks over at Pete and laughs again. " You're a little nervy today. Don't worry about visibility, we're safe. I can tell where we are with the instruments. I could stay up here forever, especially on a day like this. Look." They are still high enough to have clouds below them; little, unserious clouds that trundle along as though they are heading off to a school where they will learn what clouds should truly be. Below them is smoke, and flame, and – when the air current happens to sweep strongly in one direction – the solid realities of their earth. "How can anyone *not* love this?" John asks and slaps Pete's thigh.

Yes, how can anyone not? Pete does love it, there is something in it that he loves, but he cannot lescape the feeling he has today, that he never meant to come here. When you are young, he thinks, you dream, and in your mind, your dreams take you everywhere; first to the places you want to go, and then – elsewhere, to places you never meant to go at all. For him, this is elsewhere. It is like a disease that you think you are safe from because you live in a place where the disease is not known to exist. But it does. It exists everywhere.

But how can he not love it, this glimpse of heaven?

He turns to John and says, "This isn't heaven. It's just the sky."

John looks confused for a second, and then throws his head back and laughs.

" Christ, Mays, don't go philosophical on me. Shoot your fucking pictures." He takes the plane down lower, where they can feel the effects of the wind. "They'll be out soon, these fires. They aren't burning as steady as they were, even with the wind. The air's changing. It'll rain one day soon."

"There's nothing left to burn, " Pete says, trying to steady both himself and the camera while he opens the window. The urge to take pictures is returning. "The air up here is so clear. The smoke's all down there, what there is of it. Go lower."

"You ever fought one of 'em?"

"No. Have you ever?"

"Sure. Not these, but I've fought 'em out west a couple of times, where they destroy whole towns. Those fires don't give up on their own the way these do – they have to be defeated. Just my thing – I like a good fight." He winks at Pete, who isn't looking because he is focused on something he has seen.

They are flying over an area that has already burned.

"Look John, down there. Deer. Three, no, four of them. What are they doing so close to the fire? Can you go lower? But not too low. Be careful."

"Yessir." He slows the plane and brings it lower. "Lookie there. Looks like a family. I should've brought my hunting rifle, make you take the controls while I get dinner."

Pete isn't listening. They are at a good angle, and he is busy with the deer – a buck, two does and a young one, not quite a yearling, probably born early last spring. They hear the low flying plane and freeze for a moment with their heads toward the sky. Pete snaps, and then they are off, fast, through the woods.

"Shit, that idiot buck – he's leading them toward the fire." John begins to follow them. Pete shifts and begins to close the window.

"What are you closing the window for? I can get closer for a really good shot."

"That's okay, John. Let's go check out that fire. Pull up a little – we're too low. We're too low."

But John isn't listening now. His eyes are on the buck; Pete sees what he is trying to do and opens the window again in spite of himself.

"There ya go!" John shouts; he is nearly over them, just above the treetops, and the deer, slowing, look up again. It's perfect. Pete feels the thrill of knowing it is perfect and snaps.

There is a flat, inconsequential thud beneath Pete's feet, then the deer are off running again, and the camera flies out of Pete's hands. It hits the edge of the open window, hesitates as though it is considering its options, then drops resignedly out the window. Reflexively, Pete reaches, but it's too late. The scrape of branches is pronounced now – it is almost comic – but the plane resists the trees' efforts to cradle it and hold it upright.

"Oh shit," John says. Pete tries to look at him but finds he is facing in the wrong direction.

So this is what it's like, Pete thinks regretfully. His earlier panic has fled, and he is nearly gleeful with relief because he feels no pain; this is an easy business. But then he wonders what he is supposed to be thinking, given the serious constraints on what he now assumes is his remaining time. He tries to think those things, but his mind, freed at last from its moorings, resists the clutter of truisms.

He is aware as from a distance of the plane's tortured descent through the tops of the trees. He comforts himself with the thought that he has done something legendary; like Icarus he has just fallen out of the sky.

On Sunday Bella steadily weakens. Henry stays in her room, hating to leave even to go to the bathroom. Every now and then her eyes flutter open, always on him, and she smiles. He had thought, after the dance yesterday, that they would have so much to say to one another, but there is almost nothing either has to say.

It is Mary's day to work, and unwilling to be excluded as long as she is there, she comes in and out of the room making suggestions and neatening up. At three o'clock, Henry tells her she should go, that he is there and they don't need anything. She is always happy to leave. It isn't Pat's night to stay over, but having realized the day before that Bella is declining, she calls late in the afternoon. "I can come tonight if you like, Henry."

"I don't know," he says.

"You can call me," she tells him. "At any hour."

"Bella doesn't want the doctor to come. She doesn't want anything, except for me to stay with her. But could you come, and be here just in case we need you?"

As evening falls, the house begins to creak, and Henry imagines a gathering of spirits in preparation for Bella's departure, although the truth is that the barometric pressure is changing. He hears a door open and close downstairs and a few minutes later Pat appears at the doorway to let him know she's here. She doesn't come in.

Close to midnight, Bella grows restless, and Henry moves from the chair to the bed and takes her hands in his. "I'm here, dearest Bella. It's all right."

Her eye open and meet his. "Oh, Max, darling Max, " she says. "I wish we had both known then what we do now."

She is calmer after that. Henry returns to the chair, and although he doesn't mean to, he dozes. He is wakened by the utter stillness and knows immediately that she has gone. He moves again to the bed, this time reluctantly, and puts his fingers to her wrist, then her chest, and finally her lips. He sits for several minutes on the edge of the bed, one hand holding hers and the other rubbing the knee he had banged the day before. He puts down her hand and walks to the window. It is raining so lightly that he is not sure at first, and he feels a detached surprise that after so much heat and dryness the sky doesn't show more violence. But the air feels better, and the steady patter is pleasant. He goes downstairs to tell Pat.

At mid-morning, just after the men from the funeral home have left, the phone rings. It is Linda.

"Henry, have you spoken with Pete lately?" she asks without preamble.

"Not for a few days, no. Why?"

"When I got to work this morning, I heard that a plane went down yesterday somewhere over the north ridge of Kramer Valley. They say John Daley was flying it – that's Pete's friend. I had called Pete's house last night and got no answer – it didn't worry me until I heard this news. I called the school, and he hasn't shown up."

"Jesus."

"There are crews out searching for the plane. The fires are dying, thanks to the rain, but the terrain up there is rough. They could be anywhere."

"Pete might not have gone with him," Henry says unconvincingly.

"Maybe not," she responds equally unconvincingly. "Will you let me know if you hear anything? And I will do the same. Someone should go speak to Roy."

She will be the first person he has told himself – Pat called the funeral home. It hasn't seemed real up to now. He knows he must tell her, but once he has said the words, they will be unretractable. "Linda…"

"What?" She is curt, worried about Pete.

"My mother died during the night."

"Oh God, Henry, I'm so sorry. I shouldn't have bothered you – I didn't know."

"Of course not – you're the first person I've told. Pat's here. It's all right. I'll – I'll go speak to Roy. Yes, it will give me something to do. I won't tell you not to worry. I have to arrange Bella's funeral, but I'm not that busy – call me if you need help."

By the time of Bella's funeral on Wednesday, there is still no sign of the wrecked plane. Now that the skies have decided to open, they seem to have no intention of closing again; the rains have gained momentum and whereas a few days earlier the fires would have hampered searching, now the downpours are fulfilling the same function. There is no great danger of serious flooding, but the mountain creeks are running fast and there are reports of slides in places. Mostly, visibility is poor and walking unpleasant and difficult in the steep, wooded and cliff-impeded countryside.

Henry balks at having the funeral service in the sterile chapel of the funeral home and decides to call at the tiny Episcopal Church in Kramer to see if something can be arranged. The minister is a pleasant young man who has never met or even heard of Bella. "My mother was English," Henry explains rather disingenuously. "A member of the Anglican Church, which is the same as Episcopalian. I think my parents may have come here sometimes, long ago. She left no instructions, but I thought she might have liked the service to be held here.

Would you be willing?"

Many more people turn up than he expects, so that the church, which has a capacity to hold perhaps one hundred, is about half-full. Pat drives Henry, and they stop to get Roy. Linda walks over from the bank with a few of her colleagues, but when she enters the church, Henry is waiting. "I want you to sit with Roy and Pat and me," he says, and so she follows him up the aisle to the front of the church.

The service is brief and without embellishment, with the exception of one indulgence. Henry, having come so late to an appreciation of his mother's intellect, cannot resist adding a poem or two from the collection of books sent long ago from England. Not wishing to offend the nice Episcopal minister, he chooses George Herbert's *The Pulley* to read in the church. Later, by the graveside, in the rain, with only the minister, Pat, Roy, Linda, and the men from the funeral home present, he reads what to him are Coleridge's most beautiful words, only a gloss on the mariner's tale:

In his loneliness and fixedness he yearneth towards the journeying moon, and the stars that still sojourn, yet still move onward; and everywhere the blue sky belongs to them, and is their appointed rest, and their native country and their own natural homes, which they enter unannounced, as lords that are certainly expected and yet there is a

silent joy at their arrival.

He believes she would be pleased.

"They are thinking of calling off the search until the weekend," Linda tells Henry as they walk down the hillside from the gravesite. "The weather is supposed to clear before then. I've called Mary Kay, Pete's sister. She is coming down from Pittsburgh tomorrow. I'm going to go to Pete's this evening after work and do some cleaning up before she comes."

"How about my helping you?'

"I would like that, if you're sure…"

"I'm sure."

"How's Sarah doing?" he asks Roy as Pat drives them back up the valley.

"As well as can be expected. I went down to see her last weekend, and will go again this weekend. The hospital is a nice place. I never thanked you…"

"I don't deserve thanks. Arrangements should have been made a long time ago. I want to ask you something though. Max. Did you like him?"

There is a long pause before Roy speaks. "You want me to say yes. You want me to keep on doing what I did and your mother did, don't you?"

"Actually, I'd like the truth."

"Then the truth is, I don't know. I hated him sometimes – he was a right cruel bastard. But he had his qualities. There was something about him that touched my heart the way one of those old blues songs does. I always thought it funny that a mixed-up white man could do that to me."

"I want to give Sarah the house, and the money that's left." Seeing Roy's look, he adds quickly, "I'll be returning to New York as soon as possible and don't need it. I'm going to take the books and a few other things. The house could be sold, if you or she don't want to live in it."

Their good bye is brief and unemotional. There are both too many things to say, and too few.

Pat drops Henry at the foot of the walk to the house. "Call me if you need anything," she says.

"I will. When will you start your new job?"

"Monday. An old lady in Kramer. There are a lot more old ladies than old men."

He lets himself in by the back door and walks from room to room, listening, smelling, searching for her presence, or some other presence, searching for whatever substance, tangible or not, binds him to this place. There is *something* still, but already he feels the loosening of its grasp. He goes to her bedroom. Pat has stripped the bed and washed the sheets, and they lie folded on top of the pretty old quilt that covers the mattress. He sinks into the rocking chair, his rocking chair, and within five minutes is asleep.

He leaves at seven to meet Linda at Pete's house. She has parked in the pull-off below Roy's cottage, and he does the same. As he walks past Roy's, a light comes on inside, but he doesn't stop. It isn't raining, but the air is still heavy with the threat of a fresh downpour. He doesn't mind. It has been so dry for so long that it will take awhile to tire of the new state of the weather. And he loves the smell.

Linda is in the kitchen scrubbing the sink. "Boys! Such pigs!" she exclaims, attempting lightheartedness, and promptly begins to weep. Henry takes the sponge from her hand, turns off the water, and puts his arms around her. "Don't Linda, or we'll both be good for nothing."

"It's too much, isn't it? First Bella and now this."

"Yes." But the truth is, he is numb and has hardly given Pete a thought. "What do we need to do? Pete's evidence to the contrary, not all boys are slobs."

She laughs and swipes at the tears on her cheeks. "Yes, anal types like my brother and you are the stereotypical exceptions. Jack used to chastise *me* for *my* mess. " And that memory would have set her off again had Henry not hustled her into the living room.

"I'll finish scrubbing the kitchen," he says. "Why don't you go upstairs and make a bed for Mary Kay and see if the bathroom is presentable?"

He finishes scrubbing the sink and countertops quickly, then looks for a broom or a mop to use on the kitchen floor. He opens a door and hits the switch beside it, finding himself at the top of the basement stairs. That is when he thinks of Pete, of the possibility of his death, of their last time together, their last conversation, of the fact that he feels so distant from him – that he has created that distance himself, in reaction to Pete's ambivalence – and of the photographs. The photographs. Pete's darkroom is in the basement.

He descends and wanders through the unfinished space, pulling the strings on bare overhead bulbs as he passes under them, until he comes to a rough partition with a door. He switches on the light. The room is raw, utilitarian, as it ought to be, except for the beautiful photographs strewn everywhere. They aren't disorderly; it is just that there are so many of them Pete has run out of storage. Henry bends to retrieve a handful from a stack on the floor and lays them on the table. There are a dozen of them, from that day when they first met in the post office and Henry followed him to the stagnant pool where the tadpoles were. Such perfect symmetry; Pete's eye for form amid the swirl of light and shadow is uncanny. Inhuman. Except, Henry sees, the shadow of himself in one of them – just a shadow, subduing the tadpoles and their temporary habitat. He lays the photographs down and goes into the dark room where several pictures are still hanging on the line.

These are of the fires, prisms of smoke and flame, sharp as glass because they are in black and white. Henry thinks, I don't know this man. I have never known him.

"Henry?"

"Down here - in the basement," he calls.

A minute later she is beside him. "You can tell those are from his first flight," she says calmly. "There's a nervy quality to them. He was so afraid, that day!"

"He was?"

"God, he was terrified of flying. He had to make himself get past it, and he did – for this. He's completely obsessed. He was."

"He should have a show," Henry says. "Somewhere."

"Yes, he should, but I don't think it ever occurred

271

to him. We will have to do it for him. Look, he's thrown a bunch away – I wonder why." She pulls the batch of photographs out of the trashcan and lays them on the counter. Henry moves over to look.

Bach. He moves into Bella's room, avoiding the bed, avoiding the chest of drawers, avoiding thinking, but in virtuosic increments, and Pete takes a picture. He poses, statuesque as a god, vulnerable and silly as a child, in the center of the room, and Pete snaps. They laugh. Henry takes off his shirt, pliés, pushes Pete toward the sofa, pirouettes. Pete doesn't know the terms; what do the terms matter? They are words, in a foreign language. Henry backs off – listens – he can't resist the C-minor, he loves the steps he has created, Pete kneels, snaps, says his name...

"Henry? Henry, these are...oh, my god." Linda is ruffling through the photographs, having a quick glimpse at each, just enough to reinforce the impact of the previous one. He steps back, watching her. His customary detachment allows him to track her movements, but in slow motion: her big hands, honey-toned and reluctant, shuffle the stack of pictures and group them into a weapon which she lifts and would hit him with, except that choreography is his gift, not hers: he grabs her wrists, extracts the pictures and throws them onto the counter, pulls her to him, just close enough to unnerve her, and says, "Stop."

He takes her upstairs, to the kitchen. They sit at the table, with its formica top. She presses her elbows into the table, and her head into her hands. Henry waits.

"You. First you took Jack, then you took Pete. I never even dreamed!"

"What do you mean, I took Jack?" Henry is as stunned as she is.

"Oh, nothing. It wasn't your fault. But it would have been so much easier if he hadn't announced his love for you to our parents!" Her innate kindness kicks in then and she looks him in the eye for the first time since they came up from the basement. "Oh nevermind. But Henry – Pete?"

He can think of nothing to say. He doesn't want to think of anything. He doesn't want to think and he doesn't want to talk, so he sits there with his eyes closed and shakes his head. Then he is struck with the memory of words he spoke to Pete the last time they were together. *Can't you love me, and love Linda too, in whatever way you do, without it becoming some sort of moral statement?* But it is a hollow echo now, a glib excuse for self-indulgence. He starts to tell her that when there is a clatter and a fumbling at the kitchen door. They look up.

The door opens, and the drenched, tattered, burned, and hungry figure who is Pete stands before them. For the briefest of instants the world halts, and hangs wavering like a vapor in the air, then he moves forward into his own kitchen. "We crashed," he says, "right on the edge of the fire. I tried to get John out. I think he was dead, the way his eyes looked. I lost my camera. It was hot. His legs were caught. And then I got lost. I just walked. I walked." Henry and Linda have both risen. Pete looks from one to the other of them, and then, with a wild ecstatic look on his face and an inept lurch forward, folds himself into Linda's ample arms.

EPILOGUE

His father had been an Appalachian coal miner's son who returned from the Ardennes a different man. His mother was the daughter of English merchants with pretenses to the aristocracy, who had given her books and her identity but not her mind, after all, to an abusive husband. But does that describe them, either of them, or their roles in his development? And then there are all the other comrades and acquaintances of his youth, finally little more than pencil outlines of his own various aspects. He doesn't miss them.

Years later, Henry looks back with amazement upon the tidiness of those three months, forgetting that they did not seem so tidy at the time. From a distance, he can see how clearly his arrival and departure were not only delineated but ordained, and is thankful to have been granted so much insight.

What for him appears in retrospect as a compact, isolated, and invaluable interval is for others only a tiny fragment of ongoing existence –he has the advantage in being a person who returned to a place he had left. Roy lives another two years without revealing to anyone either that he has a heart condition or that he continues to resent the parameters his race, his era, and his own character have forced upon him – and that is aside from his concern about Sarah. She survives him by only another two years, institutionalized, while the house Henry gave her sits empty and deteriorating.

Pete and Linda live in Pete's house, and no one can say what their marriage is except themselves, who choose not to. Ruthie leaves, as Henry did, as Mary Kay did, and does well in her new life – like them, she rarely returns home. After ten years of Christmas cards, Henry looses touch with them. His point of reference and his reality are no longer the world of his youth and adolescence, although his work might sometimes indicate otherwise, and it is acclaimed in nearly all the capitols of the world.

The dream that used to haunt him has never recurred. He sometimes thinks of it but no longer feels its weight at all; he can remember that it frightened him, but not the sensation of fear. He has always assumed that the shadow-man on the train was Max, but he sees now that the person locked inside the dream was his half-sister Sarah, not himself. It is only that which makes him sad.

The end.

C.P.T. (Caroline) Jennings is a native Appalachian who makes her home in Manhattan.

www.ingramcontent.com/pod-product-compliance
Lightning Source LLC
Chambersburg PA
CBHW070922260626
47162CB00007B/2766